THE DUKE COMES HOME

Barbara Cartland

Barbara Cartland Ebooks Ltd

This edition © 2018

ISBNs

9781788671132   EPUB

9781788671149   PAPERBACK

Book design by M-Y Books
m-ybooks.co.uk

THE BARBARA CARTLAND ETERNAL COLLECTION

The Barbara Cartland Eternal Collection is the unique opportunity to collect all five hundred of the timeless beautiful romantic novels written by the world's most celebrated and enduring romantic author.

Named the Eternal Collection because Barbara's inspiring stories of pure love, just the same as love itself, the books will be published on the internet at the rate of four titles per month until all five hundred are available.

The Eternal Collection, classic pure romance available worldwide for all time .

THE LATE DAME BARBARA CARTLAND

Barbara Cartland, who sadly died in May 2000 at the grand age of ninety eight, remains one of the world's most famous romantic novelists. With worldwide sales of over one billion, her outstanding 723 books have been translated into thirty six different languages, to be enjoyed by readers of romance globally.

Writing her first book 'Jigsaw' at the age of 21, Barbara became an immediate bestseller. Building upon this initial success, she wrote continuously throughout her life, producing bestsellers for an astonishing 76 years. In addition to Barbara Cartland's legion of fans in the UK and across Europe, her books have always been immensely popular in the USA. In 1976 she achieved the unprecedented feat of having books at numbers 1 & 2 in the prestigious B. Dalton Bookseller bestsellers list.

Although she is often referred to as the 'Queen of Romance', Barbara Cartland also wrote several historical biographies, six autobiographies and numerous theatrical plays as well as books on life, love, health and cookery. Becoming one of Britain's most popular media personalities and dressed in her trademark pink, Barbara spoke on radio and television about social and political issues, as well as making many public appearances.

In 1991 she became a Dame of the Order of the British Empire for her contribution to literature and her work for humanitarian and charitable causes.

Known for her glamour, style, and vitality Barbara Cartland became a legend in her own lifetime. Best remembered for her wonderful romantic novels and loved by millions of readers worldwide, her books remain treasured for their heroic heroes, plucky heroines and traditional values. But above all, it was Barbara Cartland's overriding belief in the positive power of love to help, heal and improve the quality of life for everyone that made her truly unique.

AUTHOR'S NOTE

The ancestral homes in England thrill every tourist because so many of them are still lived in by their owners. Only by opening them to the public can they pay the rates, taxes, upkeep and repairs, which rise astronomically every year.

But what a joy and delight it is to see a house complete with its treasures collected over the centuries and know that it is still a home. In France the Châteaux are empty and in other parts of Europe only museums.

In England the Duke of Marlborough, descendant of the Great Duke, still lives at Blenheim Palace. The Earl Spencer, father of Diana, Princess of Wales, is the ninth Earl to live at Althorp and he and his wife, who is my daughter, are nearly always there at weekends to welcome the sightseers.

At Longleat, the attractive Marquis of Bath and his family show their visitors round and so does the Marquis of Tavistock who follows the example set by his father, the Duke of Bedford, at Woburn Abbey.

The National Trust owns and preserves more than two hundred historic buildings and they are visited annually by nearly five million people.

The Nizam of Hyderabad, at one time reputed to be the richest man in the world, owned the most fabulous jewels. The diamonds came from his own mines, among them the famous Koh-i-Noor, which is now incorporated in the Crown of England.

CHAPTER ONE
1875

" – to my only surviving child, my daughter Ilina, the Nizam's jewels."

The voice stopped and Mr. Wicker, the Solicitor, put down on the table the legal documents that he had been reading from.

Lady Ilina Bury stared at him in such surprise that her eyes seemed to fill the whole of her small face.

"Is that – all?" she asked in a voice that quivered.

Mr. Wicker found it difficult to look at her.

"I am afraid, Lady Ilina, that your father altered his will a year before he died. I argued with him at the time and hoped that it was just a passing phase, but then as you know he became unapproachable."

"Just the – Nizam's jewels!" Lady Ilina murmured beneath her breath.

Then the words seemed to burst from her lips as she added,

"He hated me! He hated me violently from the moment David was killed, so I suppose I might have expected something like this to happen."

"Although I cannot believe," Mr. Wicker answered, "that your father really hated you, if I am frank I would say that from the moment your brother died, his brain became a little deranged."

Ilina nodded.

She knew that this was the truth and that her father was so desperately unhappy when his only son and heir was killed in Egypt in what was not even a battle but just a skirmish between British troops and some rebellious natives that he was no longer himself.

And yet she could hardly believe that the only thing he had left her in his will was something that did not in reality exist.

The Nizam's jewels were a legend in the Bury family and it had amused Ilina and her brother David when they were children to search for them in the huge rambling house.

All that was known was that when in 1805 the Marquis of Bury returned from India where he had been serving under Sir Arthur Wellesley, he brought with him what was reported to be a fabulous and extremely valuable collection of jewels that had been given to him by the Nizam of Hyderabad.

History related that he had saved the Nizam's life and in gratitude had been rewarded with huge diamonds from the Nizam's own mines as well as emeralds, rubies, sapphires and inevitably large strings of pearls, which would be worth a fortune.

The Marquis, who had later become the second Duke of Tetbury, was, however, already a rich man and he had given them to his wife for safekeeping until the war was over.

When his father died in 1812 and he inherited the title, he set his estates in order and decided that he must fight again under the Duke of Wellington, who was now advancing into France with a large Army.

He was apparently welcomed by the great Duke with open arms, only unfortunately to be killed at the Battle of Waterloo.

It was a generation later that it was learnt from his letters, which had been kept by the Duchess, what had happened to the jewels.

In one of them he wrote,

> *"I would be worried my dearest wife, that you might be in fear of robbers and thieves had I not hidden the Nizam's jewels in such a clever way that it would be impossible for any outsider to find them. Be very careful therefore not to mention where they are to any member of the household for, even though our servants have been with us for a long time, greed can sometimes undermine loyalty and, as we both already know, that particular treasure is worth a great deal of money."*

He then went on to describe his activities as a soldier and there was no mention in that letter or any of his others of where the jewels had been hidden.

The Duchess died soon after her husband it was said of a broken heart, but either she did not have time or did not wish to confide to anybody where the jewels were hidden.

The story of their magnificence had intrigued and excited the children of each succeeding Duke and Ilina and her brother had been no exception.

Often when it rained David would say to her,

"Today we will go treasure hunting and I will bet you two sweets to one that we will find first the diamonds and then the rest of the spoils."

The way he spoke always made Ilina feel that she was betting on a certainty only to find herself at the end of the day the recipient of his sweets while the treasure still evaded them.

Now, as she looked at Mr. Wicker in despair, she thought that despite the size of Tetbury Abbey they had over the years searched every nook and cranny from the attics to the cellars.

In fact she had long ago begun to suspect that the jewels either had never existed or had been stolen long ago.

That her father, whom she had tried to love, should have left her nothing else in his will was not only insulting but in his own rather cruel way was telling her how much he resented that he had no heir.

"Why were you not a boy?" he had asked furiously after David was killed.

Then in a different tone he shouted,

"I must be married. I am not too old to beget another son. Find me a wife. God damn you, there must be some woman who will have me!"

That he was crippled and unable to leave his bed would have made him an object of pity if he had not been so intensely disagreeable and so often cruel to Ilina that at times she felt that she would rather be dead like her brother.

Her father, the fifth Duke, had lived his life fully, handicapped only by the restriction of not having enough money.

When a fall out riding left him partially paralysed and unable to move unless he was carried, he railed against Fate.

He then found life so intolerable that the only solace he could find was in drinking until his fingers were distorted with gout.

Alcohol, however, did not make him merry but merely more aggressive and, as Ilina was the only person who would stay with him and tolerate his behaviour, she found herself enduring a life of such misery that, although she was unwilling to admit it, her father's death was a merciful release.

And yet now he was stretching out beyond the grave to hurt her again.

Because she had known the grey-haired Solicitor all her life she said after a moment,

"What – can I do – Mr. Wicker?"

"I have lain awake asking myself that very question, Lady Ilina," he replied, "and to be honest, I have not found an answer."

Ilina rose to her feet and walked to the window to stand gazing out, not seeing the overgrown garden, the ancient oaks in the Park or the few remaining swans on the lake which would have died or flown away long ago if she had not remembered to feed them.

The sunlight touched her hair and Mr. Wicker thought as he had so often before that she was one of the loveliest girls he had ever seen.

Her gown, threadbare and out of date, did not disguise the elegant and youthful curves of her body.

He suddenly remembered with almost a start that she must be nearly twenty-one, having spent the last two years tied to a sick man's room and having practically no contact with the outside world. And no longer a girl but a woman.

Now he said a little hesitatingly,

"I suppose there is no relation who you could go and live with?"

Ilina turned from the window.

"Who?" she asked. "You know that Papa quarrelled with everybody we are related to. He disliked them even before David was killed and afterwards refused to have anything to do with them."

"Nevertheless, 'blood is thicker than water'," Mr. Wicker replied.

Ilina sighed.

"What do you think my life would be like if I foisted myself onto some distant cousin and could not even pay for the food I put into my mouth?"

Mr. Wicker's lips tightened.

"I agree it is an intolerable situation and I only wish that there were something I could do about it."

"Everything in the house and on the estate is entailed," Ilina said as if she was talking to herself, "and I suppose the only things I could claim are the few pieces of furniture that belonged to Mama and there are not very many of those."

Mr. Wicker was aware of this and said,

"There is just one thing which may help you, although I admit it is not very much."

"What is that?"

"My partners and I sold a cottage on the outskirts of the estate a year ago," Mr. Wicker explained. "I reckoned at the same time that you had spent some of the money your mother left on her death on things that were needed in the house."

Ilina was listening intently as he went on.

"As we were aware of this cruel clause in your father's will, we set aside fifty pounds of what we received for the cottage, which we considered to be yours, should necessity arise."

Ilina smiled and it made her look lovelier than she was already.

"That was very kind of you, Mr. Wicker, and I shall be very grateful for the fifty pounds. It is almost exactly the amount I spent on a new kitchen stove when the old one was burnt out and Papa refused to replace it."

She gave a little sigh before she continued,

"The rest of the money, which, as you know was less than one hundred pounds, has been spent on food, clothes and charities. The last, I regret to say, claimed a very small share."

There was a faint smile on her lips and just a fleeting glimpse of two dimples one on either side of her mouth.

Then, as she walked back towards the old Solicitor, she declared,

"So I have fifty pounds and, of course, Pegasus! He is mine and nobody can dispute that."

As Mr. Wicker knew, Pegasus was her adored horse, which her brother David had given her as a birthday present before he went abroad never to return.

He had then been only a foal, but Ilina had loved him and brought him up so that he followed her everywhere and came when she called as a child or a dog would have done.

She sat down on a chair facing the Solicitor and asked,

"What can I do? Shall I set off on Pegasus with my fifty pounds to seek my fortune or do I stay here and throw myself on the – mercy of the – new Duke?"

There was a note in her voice that told Mr. Wicker how disagreeable the second idea was to her.

"I am sure that His Grace will do his duty," Mr. Wicker replied hastily.

"Duty! Duty!" Ilina cried. "I know exactly what that means. Christian charity and the expectation that I shall grovel and be effusively grateful for every crumb he allows me."

The way she spoke made Mr. Wicker give a little laugh before he replied,

"Now, Lady Ilina, it need not be as bad as that. After all we know nothing about the new Duke and he may in fact be a charming man."

"That was not Papa's impression. He had always hated the new Duke's father and used to refer to him as my 'crooked cousin'."

"I have heard His Grace say it," Mr. Wicker admitted, "but I was never brave enough to ask the reason."

"It was something quite simple," Ilina said. "He either had charged my father too much for a horse he had bought for him or Papa suspected, without there being any foundation in fact that he cheated at cards."

She gave a little sigh as she added,

"You know what Papa was like once he had an idea in his head."

"I do indeed," Mr. Wicker agreed, "and I know that there was no love lost between His Grace and Mr. Roland Bury."

"Papa always said that his son Sheridan was a 'chip off the old block' and just as crooked and unpleasant as his father."

"You have never met your cousin Sheridan?" Mr. Wicker enquired.

"You don't suppose Papa would ever let Cousin Roland come here and his son being tarred with the same brush. Papa barred him too."

"That all happened a long time ago," Mr. Wicker pointed out in a tone that tried to be consoling. "After all the new Duke is now thirty-four or thirty-five and his father has been dead for years."

"I know that, but Cousin Sheridan has been abroad for so long I doubt if he will understand English – ways and English requirements."

The way Ilina spoke made Mr. Wicker aware that she was worrying about the estate, the pensioners and the few people they still employed who were really too old for a long day's work.

"I am sure that His Grace will not be ungenerous," he said hoping that what he was prophesying would be the truth.

"Supposing he is as hard up as I am?" Ilina asked. "I know his father did not have much money and the reason Cousin Sheridan went abroad was that he could not afford the gaieties he wished to enjoy in London."

Mr. Wicker had no reply to this. He was only thinking that it would require a very rich man to restore Tetbury Abbey to what it had been in the past.

Originally until the time of King Henry VIII it had been a Monastery. Then every successive owner had added to it and altered it until it was difficult to believe that there had ever been anything sanctified about the building.

Even so Ilina often imagined that there was an air of Holiness about the Chapel, although it had been rebuilt and the cloisters, which had been preserved even when the rest of the house had been altered.

The first Duke had employed the leading architect of his time to practically rebuild the house altogether and its Palladian appearance was very impressive.

And yet there were parts dating from Queen Anne, Charles II and even Queen Elizabeth tucked away behind the great facade which made it, Ilina thought, very lovable and different from anybody's else's ancestral home.

Whatever her difficulties and unhappiness with her father, she had always felt as if she was part of The Abbey, that it protected her and as long as she was underneath its roof nothing could really harm her.

And yet now a stranger had inherited it, a stranger who was coming here to take her father's place and every instinct in her rebelled against asking him to support her.

'What can I do?' she asked herself wildly and knew that Mr. Wicker was asking the same question.

Aloud she said,

"I shall have to find employment of some sort."

"That is impossible."

"Why?"

"I could give you a number of reasons," Mr. Wicker replied. "The first is because you are who you are, and secondly you are far too lovely to earn your living in any way and to attempt to do so would be dangerous."

"Dangerous?" Ilina queried.

Then she said,

"I suppose you are thinking that I might be – pursued or – insulted by men."

"Of course I think that," Mr. Wicker answered, "and you know that, if your mother was alive, by this time you would have made your curtsey to the Queen and had a Season in London. And doubtless by now you would be married."

Ilina laughed and it was a very musical sound like the song of a bird.

"Oh, Mr. Wicker, you are a romantic! And even if Mama had been alive, I doubt if there would have been enough money for a Season in London and, if there are any eligible bachelors in this part of the world, I have yet to meet them."

"You have not had the chance."

As that was an indisputable fact, Ilina did not argue.

She only thought of how gloomy it had been, hour after hour, day after day, month after month, tending a sick man who growled and shouted at her and who refused to allow anybody to come into the house.

Her father had always been quarrelsome and after his accident he had a horror of being seen or pitied.

Looking back Ilina could only remember the doctor and Mr. Wicker and occasionally a local farmer or two ever coming to see her.

"It has been very depressing," she said frankly, "but I cannot see that things will be very much better if I have to live in one of the cottages in the village. Fifty pounds will not keep me from starving for ever and I have to feed Pegasus."

The urgency in her voice when she mentioned her horse was very obvious and Mr. Wicker answered,

"Yes, of course. We must not forget Pegasus."

Then, as if he had made up his mind, he bent forward to say earnestly,

"Quite frankly, Lady Ilina, there is nothing you can do but stay here and, as there is nobody but you to run the house and the estate, I feel that the new Duke will find you very useful."

"I doubt it. If he is like most people he will be a new broom wanting to sweep clean and the last thing he will want is somebody like me hanging round his neck and telling him how things were done in the past."

The Solicitor did not reply and after a moment she asked him,

"There is not much – alternative – is there?"

"I am afraid not and quite frankly, Lady Ilina, you cannot be here on your own, as you must be well aware."

"I shall be twenty-one in a month's time."

"Even at that great age," Mr. Wicker said with a smile, "you cannot live by yourself or as you suggest, earn your own living."

"It is really ridiculous, is it not," Ilina asked, "that although I am well educated and without being conceited very well read, I cannot earn anything with my talents."

"Ladies are not expected to earn their own living."

"I am sure that most ladies enjoy playing the piano, sketching and entertaining their friends," Ilina said, "but those comforts are what I cannot afford."

Mr. Wicker sighed.

"I am afraid then you will have to ask the new Duke to look after you. After all that is what is expected of the Head of the Family."

Ilina gave a little start.

"I have not really been thinking of him as the Head of the Family. Do you think when he arrives that the cousins and the other relations I have not seen for years will gather round him and perhaps also make demands on his purse?"

"If so, I can only hope it is a large one!" Mr. Wicker said a little cynically.

Ilina jumped up again from the chair where she was sitting.

"I will not do it! I could not bear to be an encumbrance on anybody else, least of all on somebody whom Papa hated!"

As she spoke, she could hear him raving wildly from his bed,

"Do you realise that Roland's son will reign here in my place and they are both as crooked as corkscrews! Roland I loathe and detest. He always cheated when we were at Eton. I would not be surprised if he was instrumental in having David killed."

"Please – Papa," Ilina had pleaded, "you must not say such things. You know they are not true."

"*I hate him*! I hate them both!" her father had shouted, "and that damned son of his, who has been skulking about in some obscure part of the world and is doubtless riddled with opium and vice, will wear my coronet."

As her father had not worn his coronet for more than ten years, Ilina could not understand why this should perturb him.

But he referred to it again and again and assumed that since Sheridan Bury had lived in the East he took opium and indulged in every sort of exotic vice.

It was impossible when her father raved on and on not to create a picture in her mind of somebody debauched and horrible in every possible way.

Although she told herself that it was foolish and entirely lacking in substantiation, she could not help being afraid of what the new Duke would be like.

She had written to him, when the doctors had told her that it was unlikely her father would last many more months, to ask him to come home.

It had been very difficult to trace his whereabouts, but finally Mr. Wicker had been in touch with the Bank nearest to the house where Sheridan's father used to live and they had given him an address in India.

Ilina told her cousin in her letter that her father was dying and, as he was the heir to the Dukedom, it would be wise for him to come home.

She had written simply and she hoped pleasantly.

Because she had made a great effort to be as nice as possible, she had resented the fact that Sheridan Bury had neither answered her letter nor acceded to her suggestion that he should return.

It was easy enough to excuse him on the ground that he might not have received the letter.

But as she had addressed it care of the Bank, she could not believe that it would not reach him eventually. Was he in fact not interested in his future prospects?

Since the opening of the Suez Canal in 1869, instead of taking as much as three months to reach India, it was now possible for a ship to travel from Bombay to England in just under twenty days.

Her father had lingered for six months after the doctors' announcement that there was nothing more they could do for him and now nearly three weeks after his funeral there was still no sign of the new Duke.

Because it was impossible to sit still Ilina once again walked across the room.

Then, as she looked up at one of the pictures of her ancestors on the wall, she told herself that it was impossible for her to go away and leave The Abbey.

How could she abandon everything that was familiar and the only home she had ever known to enter a frightening world where she would be completely alone and practically penniless?

No, however humiliating it might be, she would stay.

Then it suddenly struck her that it might not be a matter for her to decide. The question was whether the Duke would want her in the house.

It was something that had not occurred to her before and she knew that even if he gave her a small yearly allowance she would still not know what to do or where to go and would be terrified of being alone.

It was really frightening to realise how little she knew about her relations since her father had cut off communication with them.

She was not even certain which of the older ones were still alive while the only two cousins who had come to the funeral had been old men of her father's age, who were, as it happened, both widowers.

The late Duke had married first a woman, who for some reason the doctors could not ascertain, was incapable of producing a child.

She had died when he was fifty and he had then married a very sweet and lovely person, who had not been married before because her fiancé had died unexpectedly a week before their wedding.

The two bereaved people had fallen in love with each other and in their own way had been happy even though the bridegroom often had difficulty in controlling his temper and only his wife was capable of coaxing him out of one of his black moods.

The new Duchess had been thirty-eight when she married and she produced two children, David, the boy who was born a year after their Wedding and then Ilina, who was born a year later.

The Duke had been so thrilled at having a son that as the servants often said,

"The sun rises and sets on Master David."

Everything centred round David and his whole training and upbringing was for the time when he would take his father's place and become the sixth Duke.

Unfortunately soon after the children were born things began to go wrong financially.

Because the third Duke had been extremely extravagant, there was not as much money available as there might have been although the house was in perfect order with two new wings, which proved eventually to be quite unnecessary, and the stables had been enlarged to take forty horses.

As to their investments, Ilina thought that while her grandfather might have been ill-advised, her father was obstinate and pig-headed enough to put money into Companies which promised 'get rich quick' results, but invariably more often sooner than later went bankrupt.

Gradually, as the years went by, they grew poorer and poorer while the house went unrepaired and there were very few horses in the huge stables.

Because, as children they were so happy and their home was both beautiful and entertaining, Ilina had never realised until after her mother's death how much skimping and pinching she had had to do.

As far as she and David were concerned, there were always horses of some sort to ride and there was fishing and boating on the lake.

There were also the woods where David would shoot pigeons and acres of fields in which there were partridge, hares and rabbits, all of which contributed to the larder in The Abbey.

She could never remember as she looked back on her childhood days when the sun was not shining or a dull moment when she had nothing to do.

It was only after her mother died just before Ilina's eighteenth birthday that her whole life changed and she realised that there was no one else to look after her father.

David was with his Regiment and after the Duke's accident life suddenly became a nightmare from which there was no escape.

At the same time the house was there and whatever the difficulties it was still home and still the place that she belonged to and she could not imagine her life without it.

Then, as her father moved towards the grave, she began to realise just how old everybody else was.

The people in the villages that belonged to the estate, whose cottages leaked because there was no money to repair them, were all old and decrepit.

The young people had all left. Since it was no longer possible to obtain employment at the 'Big House' as their fathers and grandfathers had, they had migrated to the nearest towns.

The farms had run down so that there were few cattle and the Home Farm that supplied the house was in the hands of a very old couple who could hardly manage to provide for themselves let alone their landlord.

'David will be able to change all this,' Ilina had thought confidently at first.

Then, when David was killed and her father was no longer sensible or sane, Ilina knew despairingly that the only person who could change anything would be the next Duke.

As Mr. Wicker had said, everything was entailed.

Nothing belonged personally to the present Duke in order to preserve the estate for generations that would come after him and she thought that in a way however much she was inconvenienced it was right.

The portraits that looked down at her were of Burys, who had played their parts in the history of England over the centuries.

It was almost as if they demanded that the line should be carried on and whatever was accumulated in the house by them or their ancestors before them must remain intact.

"I wish I could think of some way to help you, Lady Ilina," Mr. Wicker now said in a voice that made Ilina aware that he was very worried about her.

"I shall be – all right," she said bravely.

Equally every nerve in her body was crying out against the cruelty of her father in leaving her something that did not exist.

She knew that, if he had declared she should have a few hundreds of pounds a year in his will or even set down the sum that could be hers, the next Duke would honour it automatically.

That he had made a mockery of her inheritance in bequeathing to her something which, like Fairy Gold, could not be touched by human hands, was so hurtful that at first she could hardly comprehend that it had happened.

She knew, however, that when she was alone and had time to think it over, she would want to cry.

"I shall be all right," she said again, but she was reassuring herself rather than Mr. Wicker.

Then, as she felt a sudden restriction in her throat and tried to keep back her tears, she gave an exclamation.

"Mr. Wicker, I have an idea!"

"What is it?" he asked.

"I shall be here when the new Duke arrives, but I shall not let him know who I am."

Mr. Wicker looked puzzled.

"What do you mean?"

"I have to earn money. On that you must agree."

"I have told you, Lady Ilina, that it is impossible for you to do so."

"Yes, I know, but you must also admit that what I have been spending my time doing could be listed under a number of categories. In the past, when my grandfather was alive, many different people were employed in carrying them all out."

"I don't understand."

"Then listen. First there was a Librarian and a Curator. That was two posts and what they were each paid is set down in the accounts for the period. Next there was an Agent, in fact two, who looked after the estate and you can count that as another post. Then there was the housekeeper rustling I am sure in black silk with the chatelaine at her waist. She too was paid. Under her there were quite a number of housemaids who received some remuneration or other."

Ilina drew in her breath and went on,

"There was also a personal secretary who saw to Grandpapa's private correspondence, which Mama told me was always very considerable and included many *billets-doux* from beautiful women because he was so handsome."

The Solicitor laughed,

"That is true. My father always said that the Duke was the best-looking man he had ever seen."

"I have not yet finished," Ilina continued. "Looking up the accounts which were kept meticulously by his secretary, I see that there was a Major Domo who acted as a Groom-of-the-Chambers and The Abbey had two seamstresses, of whom one concentrated entirely on repairs, mending the curtains and upholstery."

Ilina paused.

Then with a smile threw out her arms,

"All those people, all employed and all paid, all part of the household, you see in one person, Mr. Wicker, me!"

Mr. Wicker stared at her.

"What are you saying?" he asked.

"I am saying that when the Duke arrives, he is going to find me indispensable at least until he can fill these posts, which are what this house and the estate require."

The Solicitor still looked bewildered and Ilina went on,

"What you have to do is promise me on your honour that you will not reveal to him who I am and, of course, I can make old Mr. and Mrs. Bird agree to do anything I ask."

"It's impossible!" Mr. Wicker said firmly.

"So impossible that it is what is going to happen," Ilina said determinedly. "Do you not see, it will save me from humiliation? And even if he decides to get rid of me, if he is a gentleman, the least he will do will be to reimburse me for the years I have spent here."

She paused before she added more slowly,

"Even if he turns out to be as parsimonious as Papa said he was, he will have to give me at least a year's wages, which is better than nothing."

"You cannot do such a thing!" Mr. Wicker objected.

"I can and I will!" Ilina asserted. "I want to stay at The Abbey, of course I do, but I also do *not* wish to hold out a begging bowl to the new Duke almost before he has set foot in his new home. I shall inform him that I am indispensable and hope he will find me so."

"But Lady Ilina," Mr. Wicker pleaded, "it would be impossible for you to stay here unchaperoned in such circumstances."

Ilina put back her head and laughed.

"Now you are looking at it from an entirely different angle. It would be much more reprehensible for me to live here with a very distant cousin as myself! But if I am just a senior servant, there is no reason why he should even notice me, except to give me orders, which is exactly what I want."

Mr. Wicker looked at her and thought that it would be impossible for any man not to notice her as a woman.

There was a worried expression on his face as he said,

"Please listen, Lady Ilina. This is something you should not do and cannot do. Be sensible and tell the new Duke who you are, in which case, as I said before, you should be chaperoned. And in no circumstances must you pretend to be of no consequence."

"I cannot understand why that should worry you," Ilina replied.

Mr. Wicker realised how innocent and unworldly she was, but he could not for the moment think of how he could put into words what he was thinking.

Then he told himself that it was very unlikely that the new Duke would be the sort of man who would be interested in what Ilina had called a 'senior servant'.

Thinking back Mr. Wicker remembered stories of Noblemen who had pursued defenceless Governesses in large houses or who enjoyed seducing girls from the villages who were foolish enough to think that it was an honour to be noticed by a member of the aristocracy.

No one knew better than he did how unsophisticated Lady Ilina was, having lived the life of a recluse ever since she had grown up.

She was telling the truth when she said that she rarely if ever met a man and he was certain the only ones she had met were himself, the doctor and the old Vicar who was doddery and half-blind.

Thinking his thoughts out loud he carried on,

"There is no reason for you to assume that the new Duke is not a gentleman. After all as a Bury he is extremely well-born."

Ilina smiled.

"According to the history of the family, there were Burys and Burys and some of them behaved abominably. But as you say, we must just hope that the new Duke is different, although Papa actually tried to convince me that he is the Devil in disguise!"

Mr. Wicker held up his hands in horror.

"You cannot risk it. Lady Ilina. Please change your mind and go to one of your relatives."

"Which one?" she asked, "and where are they? You know as well as I do that none of them came to the funeral except for those two old cousins. I have a feeling that the great majority of them are dead."

"I will make it my duty to put investigations in hand to find them," Mr. Wicker said, "wherever they may be."

"If you do, you will then try to blackmail me into going to live with one of them. Well, I will not do so!"

There was silence and then she said after a moment,

"The Abbey is my home and it is all I have left. If Pegasus and I have to go away, then I think I shall either drown myself in the lake or else die of homesickness."

She looked up at the picture of her great-great-grandfather that hung on the wall over a desk where her father had always sat and her grandfather and great-grandfather before him.

'I belong here,' she affirmed silently, 'and if Mr. Wicker is afraid for me, you will look after me.'

As she spoke with her eyes on the portrait, which badly needed cleaning, she realised that she was addressing the Duke who had hidden the Nizam's jewels before he went out to fight for his country and die.

With a smile on her lips she went on to the portrait,

'The least you could do at this moment is to tell me where you have hidden your treasure. I do not think all down the years since you were alive that there has been anybody who needed it as badly as I do now.'

The handsome face of the second Duke was, however, impassive and after a moment, almost as if she had expected him to speak, she turned away petulantly to add,

'Well, if you will not help me, I will have to help myself and that is exactly what I intend to do.'

"He might help you to see sense," Mr. Wicker came in unhappily.

"This *is* sense," Ilina replied, "because at least here in The Abbey I have a roof over my head, a bed I can sleep on and unless, the new Duke is really poverty-stricken, a crust of bread to gnaw."

She laughed and for the first time since she had heard her father's will there was a light in her eyes as she said,

"After all it will be an adventure and a change from the dismal monotony of the last two years."

CHAPTER TWO

Ilina was mending one of the curtains in the Duke's study.

The lining had split near the ground so she was sitting on the floor stitching it back into place afraid that even her delicate sewing would make the material, which was old and fragile, split again.

Because the curtains were becoming dusty she was wearing a housemaid's overall over her gown and a piece of white muslin tied over her hair.

She was thinking as she worked that this room at any rate, which was the only that one she kept open, looked attractive.

There were two huge vases of daffodils, which she had picked the day before, and which had just come into full golden bloom, and the sunshine illuminated the pictures on the wall, the china and the fine old furniture that she polished whenever she had the time.

In this room, which had been known for generations as the 'Duke's study', there were portraits of the first four Dukes of Tetbury, while her father's portrait hung in the dining room.

Every Duke had been painted when he had inherited The Abbey and the most impressive and elaborate was the picture of the second Duke, who had hidden the Nizam's jewels.

Because, as Ilina told herself, he had been very conscious of his own importance he had taken the best place behind the huge flat-topped Georgian desk and his frame was more elaborately finished than those of the other Dukes.

In fact he was the only one surmounted with the Ducal strawberry-leafed coronet and his name was embellished at the base of the picture on a scroll that was held up by small gilded angels.

Because now she found herself often thinking of him, she was wondering if he realised how drastically the house had been altered since his return to it from India and what the present Duke would think when he arrived.

Or rather if he ever arrived, which she could not help thinking desperately might never happen.

It was not three months since her father's death and there had been no message from him and she had no idea if he was coming back to England or not.

Mr. Wicker who had written to inform him of her father's death had received a letter from his Bank Manager in Calcutta informing him that the letter he had written to Mr. Sheridan Bury would be handed to him at the first possible opportunity.

"This makes me think," Mr. Wicker said, "that perhaps the new Duke is not in Calcutta or even in India."

"Then where is he likely to be?" Ilina asked.

Mr. Wicker shrugged his shoulders.

"I have no idea, Lady Ilina. Although there is little substance for my thinking it, during the years that he has been abroad Mr. Bury has travelled to many parts of the East and now for all we know he may be in China or in Timbuktu!"

They both laughed and then in a different tone of voice Ilina had asked,

"How are we to exist until he returns?"

"I have discussed that question with my partners," Mr. Wicker replied, "and we think it only right as Solicitors to the estate that we should pay the pensions until His Grace arrives and advance you a little money in order to pay the wages of Mr. and Mrs. Bird and to buy food for them and yourself."

"And Pegasus!" Ilina added quickly.

"Naturally Pegasus is included," Mr. Wicker replied gravely.

"It is very kind of you, Mr. Wicker. I hate to impose on you in this way, but I do not see that there is anything else I can do. You know as well as I do that the Birds would starve if we did not look after them."

Mr. Wicker sighed before he said,

"I discussed with my partners whether it would be possible to sell something that would at least cover your immediate requirements, but they considered that it would be illegal without the new Duke's knowledge or permission."

"I can accept that and it was very understanding of you to think of it."

Ilina smiled before she added,

"I cannot think what I should have done without you, Mr. Wicker. You have been a tower of strength ever since Papa became so difficult."

Mr. Wicker looked embarrassed by her praise.

And then she said in a small voice,

"Supposing the Duke – never returns? Or prefers to – stay out East?"

"If he does, then he will have to make some arrangements about the estate," Mr. Wicker said quickly. "But there is no point, Lady Ilina, in meeting trouble halfway."

"No, of course not," Ilina agreed. "But I cannot help worrying about the future."

"Once again," Mr. Wicker answered, "I must beg you to be frank with the Duke when he arrives and tell him who you are. He must be made to understand that you are his responsibility."

"That is something I have no wish to be. I have already persuaded the Birds to address me as 'miss' rather than 'my Lady' and I am sure if I play the part well, I shall have a job for a few months at any rate. Then I shall have to think again."

Mr. Wicker's lips parted as if he would argue with her.

Then, because he knew it was hopeless he could only think, as he had thought so often before, that any man, if he had any decency, would instinctively want to protect and look after anyone so beautiful and helpless.

At the same time, as the weeks passed and there was no sign from the Duke, even he began to feel that perhaps the shortcomings which had been attributed to him by his predecessor were correct and he was not concerned with his responsibilities in England, but only with the life that he was clearly enjoying in other parts of the world.

Because Ilina was determined that, if the Duke did arrive, he would gain the best impression possible of the house and she had spent all her energies on trying to make it look attractive.

She repaired the more dilapidated curtains and hid by moving the furniture around, the places where the carpet had become so threadbare that one could see the bare boards.

The house was so large that she often felt that she was like the small Dutch boy who had put his finger in the hole in the dyke to hold back the floodwaters.

It seemed to her that no sooner had she done one room and started on another than the cobwebs were gathering in the first and the dust was grey on the floor.

She had been obliged during her father's lifetime, when he had been confined to his bed, to shut up the State rooms.

The Silver Salon, which had been the most remarkable achievement of the first Duke's restoration, was shrouded in Holland sheets.

So was the Red Drawing Room, the writing room, the Duchess's Drawing Room, the Picture Gallery, the card room, the Music Room and a whole number of other small rooms that no one had ever thought of a name for them.

She kept open the huge Baronial Dining Room because the pantry was next door to it and the kitchen was not so far away as it was from any other room.

Sometimes when she sat alone at the large table, which could seat thirty with ease, she would imagine it peopled by beautiful ladies in elaborate gowns and gentlemen wearing glittering decorations on their evening coats.

She would imagine herself joining in witty vivacious conversation and holding her own.

Sometimes in her fantasy there would be a dark handsome man whose eyes would meet hers and it would be difficult for either of them to look away.

Then, as she finished the one dish that her meal consisted of, she had carried it back to the kitchen and given the plate to Mrs. Bird to wash it up.

It was easier to do this than to have old Bird, who was getting very slow, shuffling around the table and taking so long to serve her or fetch the spoon he had forgotten that the food was cold.

"I am sure you have enough to do, Bird," she would say, "so today I will wait upon myself."

Because she did this every day it was just a formality to save the old man's face and he would reply,

"It's very kind of your Ladyship. I've the silver to clean."

If it was not the silver, which remained year in and year out in the safe, he would occasionally reply by saying that he had to go to the cellar.

As there was very little wine left and Ilina never drank anything but water, she hoped that when the Duke did come Bird would remember which bins contained the claret and which the white wine, if indeed there was anything left of either.

After the first few weeks following her father's death, when she had expected the new Duke every day, she had begun to think that he was just a myth like the Nizam's jewels and would never turn up.

She busied herself in The Abbey and saw nobody except for the old servants and occasionally Mr. Wicker.

The few neighbours they had did not call because she was in mourning, although, if ever they had attempted to be friendly during her father's lifetime, he had either refused to see them or if he did would be extremely rude.

"For all the people I see," Ilina had said to Mr. Wicker laughingly, "I might as well be on a desert island!"

It was in fact the truth.

But in her own way she was happy, far happier than when her father had been swearing and shouting at her and had kept her running about from first thing in the morning until last thing at night.

His valet, who had been with him for nearly forty years, had stayed on out of loyalty to the family and especially to Ilina.

But once the funeral was over he had told her that he wished to retire and had arranged to live with his brother, who had a small business in the nearest town about seven miles away.

"I can work when I feels like it, my Lady," he said to Ilina, "but otherwise. I'll put me feet up."

"That is what I hope you will do, Watkins. You have been marvellous and I could never have managed Papa without you. I shall miss you greatly."

"And I'll miss you, my Lady."

"I only wish I could reward you for all your kindness and for everything you have done these past years," Ilina said in a low voice, "but as you know, I have no money at the moment. If I ever do find the Nizam's jewels, then I promise that you will be the very first person who will benefit."

"That's very kind of your Ladyship," Watkins replied, "but I'll be all right. My brother'll look after me, though I'm not sayin' as how I wouldn't have liked to have saved a bit, seein' as I've been in service since I were twelve."

"It is absolutely wrong that Papa should not have left you something in his will," Ilina said, "but – "

"Now don't you go worryin' yourself," Watkins interrupted. "When your ship comes home, my Lady, or you find them jewels, which I very much doubts, then I'd just like to hear about it for old time's sake."

"I promise you that you shall," Ilina replied.

When she said 'goodbye' to him and watched him drive away in the carrier's cart, a shabby little old man with only a small battered trunk that contained all his worldly possessions, she felt the tears gather in her eyes.

'How could Papa have forgotten him?' she asked.

She was determined, if she did nothing else, to extract some money from the new Duke both for Watkins and for the Birds.

They had been at The Abbey for nearly as long as Watkins had and they had been there long before Ilina was born and Bird had risen from being knife boy to pantry boy and from pantry boy to footman before finally he became butler.

'This is their home too,' Ilina told herself.

She knew that if the new Duke sent them away they would feel as if they had lost everything that was familiar and dear to them.

The rooms they occupied off the kitchen contained the few personal objects that they had accumulated down the years.

There was the first present that Ilina had given Mrs. Bird when she was four and had drawn her a picture of the house with two Noah's Ark figures standing in front of it, which were meant to be Bird and his wife.

There was a little purse that she had knitted another year and laboriously sewn onto it a button so that it could be closed.

There were things that Bird had collected, such as a fox's brush that her father after a particularly good hunt had had mounted and then in a fit of unusual generosity had given to Bird as a souvenir.

There was the first bow and arrow he had made for David, which he had later discarded in favour of a gun.

Bird had also preserved his first cricket bat and the ball, which had gone through the greenhouse for which misdemeanour he had been severely punished.

There were dozens of small things that Ilina knew had made the Birds feel that they were part of the family.

She had lain awake at night wondering frantically how she could explain their importance to the Duke.

'It will be easier for me to ask for money if he does not think I am family,' she told herself, 'and therefore trying to get something personal out of him.'

Even as she thought of it the idea made her hackles rise and as the days and weeks went by without her hearing from the Duke she began to hate him as her father had done.

She finished mending the lining and realised as she cut off the thread that the braid on the edge of the curtain also needed attention.

She looked at the clock on the mantelpiece and was thinking that she just had time to mend it when the door opened.

She thought that it must be Bird coming in to tell her that it was one o'clock.

Then to her surprise a man entered the room and looked round it until he saw her sitting on the floor staring at him.

Ilina was wondering if she had seen him before and if she should ask him what he wanted, when sharply in a voice that was authoritative and at the same time had a note of irritation in it, he asked,

"Where are the servants? There appears to be nobody about, not even in the kitchen!"

"There should be somebody there," Ilina replied. "What do you want?"

"Why are there no footmen in the hall?" the newcomer demanded in the same sharp almost aggressive tone of voice.

"Footmen?"

"My father told me that there were always several on duty."

It suddenly struck Ilina that this must be the new Duke and for a moment she could not believe it.

For one thing he did not look in the least like what she had expected, thinking that because he was a relation he would have some resemblance to David or to her father.

Instead he was taller, more broad-shouldered and had a handsome but unusual face in which she could see no resemblance to any of the other members of the family.

His hair was dark and his eyebrows, perhaps because he was annoyed, seemed almost to meet across his forehead. And there was something alert and vital about him that was different.

What was more, his clothes, which he wore casually as if they were of no consequence, were certainly not those of a gentleman of standing.

One glance told her that whatever else he might be, the new Duke was not a rich man.

Because his question remained unanswered and so she said after a perceptible pause,

"There have not been footmen in the hall for at least ten years."

"Why not?"

"Because there has been no money to pay for them."

The new Duke frowned and it made him look more ferocious than he did before.

Slowly Ilina rose to her feet trying to think of what she must say and how she must behave.

Because she was quite certain from the way he had spoken that he thought her to be the servant she appeared to be, she took off her apron and removed the piece of muslin that had covered her hair.

"Who are you?"

By the time this question arrived, Ilina had had time to remember the part that she had decided to play.

Carrying the apron over her arm she walked towards him to say,

"I think you must be the new Duke. Welcome, Your Grace, to Tetbury Abbey."

She dropped him a small curtsey as she spoke and added before he could reply,

"My name is Jane Ashley and I am at the moment the Curator."

"And in addition to those duties," the Duke remarked, "you also mend the curtains?"

"There is nobody else to do so, Your Grace."

He looked at her, she thought, as if he suspected that she was not telling him the truth and then he said,

"Now I am here, I think the best thing for me to do is to see the housekeeper or whoever is in charge of the house and after that perhaps you would oblige me by sending me the Estate Manager."

Ilina repressed a smile before she replied,

"Certainly, Your Grace. But perhaps first you would like some refreshment? And I presume you will be staying for luncheon?"

"Naturally," the Duke answered as if he thought that she was being impertinent.

"Then before I do anything else, perhaps it would be wise for me to inform the cook of Your Grace's intentions, although I am afraid that the meal will be very sparse."

Without waiting for the Duke to reply, Ilina went from the room closing the door behind her.

Only when she was outside did she start to run as swiftly as she could towards the kitchen.

There was no sign of either Bird or Mrs. Bird and she supposed that, as the Duke had found the kitchen empty, they would be sitting in their private room, resting before the strenuous task of cooking an egg or whatever else might be available for her luncheon.

She burst in on them to say,

"His Grace has arrived and he is expecting luncheon. Oh, Mrs. Bird, what can we give him to eat?"

Mrs. Bird heaved herself with difficulty out of her armchair.

"The new Duke, my Lady, I mean *miss*. Well, better late than never, that's what I always says."

"I should have been in the hall," Old Bird said, rising from the table where he had been sitting while he cleaned several small silver teaspoons.

"How could you have known that he was arriving today after all this time of waiting?" Ilina asked. "And would you believe it, His Grace enquired why there were no footmen in attendance in the hall."

She laughed because it sounded so funny, but the Birds just looked at her with a worried expression in their eyes and she knew that they were apprehensive, as she was, of the Duke.

"Have you some eggs, Mrs. Bird?" Ilina asked.

'There's three, miss," Mrs. Bird replied. "I was keepin' one for your supper – "

"Make an omelette," Ilina interrupted, "and I hope you will find that there is some cheese left or perhaps you could make a pudding of some sort."

She did not wait for Mrs. Bird to protest that it was impossible, but looked at Bird to say,

"Go down to the cellar as quickly as you can and bring up a bottle of claret and another of sherry or Madeira. There might even be a bottle of port."

"I doubt it. My – miss," Bird said, shaking his head.

Then without saying anything more as Ilina left he shuffled slowly along the passage towards the pantry, where the key of the cellar hung on a baize-covered board, while Ilina went up to her bedroom.

Anticipating the Duke's return, she had moved from the State room near her father's where she had slept all the time he was ill and had taken over the schoolroom on the other side of the house.

The bedroom where she had slept for so many years after she had left the nursery made her feel happier and more protected than in any other room in the house.

In these three rooms she had collected all the things that she believed were hers and which, if she was sent away from The Abbey, she was determined to take with her.

There was her mother's writing table and an inlaid French secretaire that she had brought with her when she married.

There were pictures that had been painted or drawn of her mother when she first married and a sketch of her father drawn by the artist prior to painting the large portrait of him that now hung in the dining room.

But more precious than anything else was a portrait of David in his uniform.

He looked very handsome and dashing with a smile on his lips and a twinkle in his eyes which, when she looked at him, made Ilina feel as if he was speaking to her.

None of these were particularly valuable, but each one meant a great deal to her and she knew that these were her own treasures, which she would let no one ever take from her.

As she entered her bedroom, she flung down the apron she was carrying and the muslin that had covered her head and ran to the mirror to look at herself.

She was horrified at how untidy her hair was and remembered that she had planned before the Duke arrived to brush it back from her forehead to make her look intellectual and certainly older than she actually was.

'If I was really a Curator, he would expect me to be at least over thirty,' she thought and tried various ways to make herself look older.

Now with her fair hair rioting in little curls round her forehead and arranged only loosely at the back of her head, she thought that she had been very reprehensible in having grown careless because the Duke had waited so long before he had put in an appearance.

She brushed her hair smoothly and twisted it into a tight chignon at the back of her head.

She stuck in the hairpins so hurriedly that several times she hurt herself.

Then she rushed across the room to take a dress from a wardrobe that she had altered in readiness for this particular occasion.

It was a gown that had belonged to her mother of green crêpe. It had at first been a crinoline, but now that these were out of fashion, Ilina had pulled back the full skirts into the semblance of a bustle leaving the front plain and she hoped much more severe.

The gown fastened at the neck and she had added a neat white muslin collar and small muslin cuffs to the sleeves.

She was now quite certain when she had it on that she looked older than she had before.

But she was not aware that the colour of the gown threw into prominence the dazzling whiteness of her skin and the gold of her hair and seemed to reflect in her eyes that it had gold lights in them like the bottom of a clear stream in the sunlight.

As she fastened the cuffs over her small wrists, she told herself that now she looked exactly as a Curator or perhaps a Librarian should.

With only a perfunctory glance in the mirror, she hurried downstairs again hoping that by this time Bird would have brought up the sherry from the cellar.

She found him in the pantry struggling to open the bottle, which was dusty with age.

As he drew out the cork, Ilina hurriedly took a small silver salver from the safe, which was open, put a wine glass onto it and found a decanter on the shelf that Bird could pour the sherry ointo.

"I ought to change, miss," he said as he filled the decanter and put in the stopper.

"Yes, you must," Ilina agreed. "I will take the sherry in for His Grace. Change and then lay the table for one."

"You'll not be eatin' with His Grace?"

"No, of course not," Ilina replied. "Don't forget. Bird, I am only the Curator and you know he never ate at the same table as Grandpapa."

"That be true, miss."

"I will come and help Mrs. Bird in the kitchen," Ilina said, "but don't let him know that I am there."

"It's not right, it's not right, my Lady!" Bird began, muttering beneath his breath.

"*Miss!*" Ilina said frantically. "Promise me that you will not forget that I am 'Miss Ashley'."

She picked up the silver salver as she spoke and started to walk from the pantry across the hall.

She could not run with the sherry in her hands. But she felt because she was agitated that her breath was coming quickly and her heart was pounding as she reached the study.

As she walked into it, she saw to her surprise that the Duke was sitting at what had been her father's desk and was going through the drawers.

There were several pieces of paper in front of him on the blotter that were embellished with the Tetbury Coat of Arms in gold and after a second's resentment at what he was doing Ilina remembered that he was entitled as the new Duke to do anything he wished.

"I am sorry to have taken so long, Your Grace," she apologised, "but the butler had to fetch the sherry from the cellar and luncheon is now being prepared for you."

She put the salver down on the desk in front of him and said,

"As Your Grace did not give us notice of your arrival, you will, of course, understand that the meal will therefore not be a very substantial one, but I will try to arrange for Your Grace to have a better dinner."

She had spoken without thinking and the Duke enquired,

"*You* will arrange? Am I to understand, Miss Ashley, that you are in charge here?"

"When the late Duke died," Ilina replied, "there was no one else to see to anything either inside or outside the house. So Mr. Wicker, the Solicitor to the estate, asked me to do what I could to keep the place in running order until Your Grace's arrival."

The Duke stared at her.

"Am I to understand," he asked in a slightly ominous voice, "that there is no money to run the house and the estate with?"

"I am sure that Your Grace will wish to see Mr. Wicker as soon as possible."

"But in the meantime I imagine that you can answer my questions."

"The answer," Ilina said slowly, "is that, when the late Duke died, he was to all intents and purposes bankrupt."

Because she disliked the way the Duke was speaking, she hoped to surprise him and succeeded.

He stared at her as if he could not believe that she was telling him the truth. Then after a moment he said,

"It cannot be possible! I have always imagined from what I had been told by my father that the place was kept in great style and that the last Duke lived as befitted his rank."

"That was true until about the last ten years of his life."

"How can you know that?" the Duke asked unexpectedly. "You can hardly have been here then."

Ilina thought quickly and then she said,

"As it happens, Your Grace, I was. My father served the Duke and I have lived on the estate ever since I was a child."

"Then I presume you can answer my questions. Have you any idea where the money has gone that should be keeping up both the house and the estate?"

"My father always said," Ilina replied, "that it was a question mostly of bad investments and of extravagances on the part of the third Duke."

"So what is left for me?" the Duke demanded bluntly.

Because of the almost contemptuous way he spoke, Ilina felt her temper rising.

Then she knew, as she looked at him, that she disliked the man who had arrived without any warning and without consideration for anybody else's feelings but his own.

Also he was apparently assessing what he had inherited only in terms of money without there being any sentiment or feelings about his new position.

"The answer to that, Your Grace," she said quietly and in a controlled voice, "is one of the most beautiful and historic houses in England and an estate that has belonged to your ancestors since the time of Queen Elizabeth. In other words for over three hundred years!"

She felt as she spoke that the Duke was surprised and there was no doubt that his voice was sarcastic as he responded,

"Thank you, Miss Ashley, for putting it so precisely. I am well aware of what you are expecting me to feel."

Ilina did not reply and he went on,

"At the same time you must appreciate that it is somewhat of a shock to find instead of a house filled with servants and running smoothly like a well-oiled machine, what I can see at a glance needs a great deal of money spent on it. And I imagine the land is in the same condition unless the farms have been in more competent hands."

Ilina felt herself stiffen before she managed to reply,

"It would perhaps have been wise, Your Grace, if when you were informed over a year ago that you would be the next Duke, you had made enquiries about the family inheritance or even better to have returned here to see the late Duke before he died and have some idea of what was needed."

The Duke did not speak and after a moment she went on,

"I understand that Lady Ilina wrote to you asking you to come back to England."

"Where is Lady Ilina? I wish to see her," the Duke snapped.

"I am afraid that her Ladyship has left for the North of England where she is staying with relatives."

"I suppose I can get in touch with her?"

"If that is your wish, I will endeavour to find her address," Ilina answered.

There was silence.

Then the Duke said,

"Now that I am here, I had better know the worst and, as I understand that you are in sole charge of the household, perhaps you will be kind enough to tell me of what it consists."

"It consists," Ilina answered, "of Bird, who has been here for over thirty-five years as the butler, Mrs. Bird who is the cook and Emily, who is very old, over eighty, and helps in the house when she is well enough to do so. And, of course, myself."

There was silence and then, as the Duke looked at her as if he could hardly believe what she had said, he asked,

"Is that all? Are you telling me the truth?"

"There is no reason, Your Grace, why I should deceive you."

"Who is in charge of the estate?"

There was a distinct silence before Ilina answered,

"As there is no Agent or manager, I have been looking after it for the time being. The only men employed are Jacobs, the Head Groom, although he has no one under him, and Williams, who was Head Gardener, but is at the moment crippled with arthritis, although he should be able to do a little more when the weather turns warmer."

"I cannot believe it!" the Duke exclaimed.

He brought his clenched fist down on the table to say,

"Why the hell was I not informed of this state of affairs?"

"You were," Ilina retorted angrily. "As I have told Your Grace, Lady Ilina wrote to you and asked you to come home."

"Because her letter was addressed to the wrong place and I was in a different country, I finally received it only about two weeks before I learnt of the Duke's death. Surely somebody with any sense could have communicated with me earlier than that?"

"But you must have been aware after the death of the Marquis that – you were the – heir presumptive?"

Although she was not aware of it, there was a distinct tremor in her voice as she spoke of David.

It was always agonising to realise that she would never see him again and that the house he had loved and had meant so much to him was to go to a stranger.

Despite the fact that she was feeling angry with him, Ilina thought that in a way she could understand the shock her revelations had been to the new Duke.

If, as she suspected, he had no money, it must be horrifying to find that his new possession would be nothing more than a millstone round his neck, dropping him into a deeper financial despondency than he might be in already.

'No man could look as he does if he was prosperous,' she thought.

In a softer and more gentle voice than she had used before she said,

"I am sorry if it all seems so disappointing, but I promise you that, while there was nothing that could be done until you returned, now you are back, I think money can be raised in one way or another at least to make things a little better than they are now."

There was a pause before the Duke said almost grudgingly,

"As you appear to be the only person who I can discuss these things with, you had perhaps better tell me how you think I can raise money when everything, unless I am very much mistaken, is entailed onto a son I do not yet possess?"

Because there was a sarcastic note in his voice, Ilina felt that she disliked him more every moment they were together.

"Perhaps, Your Grace," she replied, "it would be best to wait until you have had luncheon to learn the whole sad story. My Nanny always told me that things seem worse on an empty stomach."

For the first time there was a smile on the Duke's lips as he replied,

"I can remember my Nanny saying exactly the same. But because I am a very practical methodical person, Miss Ashley, I doubt very much if what you have to tell me will be any more palatable after the meal than before it."

"I hope you are mistaken about that," Ilina answered, "and you have not yet tried the sherry, which I hope will please Your Grace."

She took the stopper out of the decanter as she spoke and filled up the glass that stood beside him.

"Will you join me?" the Duke asked surprisingly.

"No, thank you. And while Your Grace is drinking this, I will go and see if your luncheon is ready."

"I should have thought the butler might have announced it," the Duke replied.

She pretended not to hear him and went from the room to run down the passage once again as hastily as she could to the pantry.

"Is luncheon ready?" she asked.

"It will be, in a minute or two, my L – miss," Bird answered, stumbling once again over the way he addressed her.

Ilina was, however, already hurrying on to the kitchen.

She knew that Mrs. Bird was a very good cook when she had the correct ingredients. At the same time, when Mr. Wicker had given her just enough money to keep them from starving during the weeks they had been waiting for the Duke, there had been no surplus for luxuries.

She had planned when the Duke did arrive to have a leg of lamb in the house and perhaps one or two young pigeons, which were always available at this time of the year.

"Can you manage, Mrs. Bird?" she asked.

"It's not what a gentleman would expect," Mrs. Bird said, "but I've made His Grace some soup from that rabbit we had yesterday and there's the omelette, which will be ready before he's finished his soup and then a bite of cheese."

She paused for breath before she went on,

"There's no time for me to make a puddin' and I meant to tell your Ladyship yesterday that we've run out of rice and there's not been sight nor sound of a ripe gooseberry in the garden yet."

Ilina blamed herself for not having looked at the gooseberry bushes instead of leaving it to Mrs. Bird.

She was quite certain that there would be some gooseberries, even though they were agonising to pick because the bushes were overgrown and, having fought one's way through the weeds and brambles, one was then scratched by the bushes. She had found it easier to say that she did not particularly like them.

'Why,' she asked herself angrily, 'could he not have let us know he was coming so that something could have been prepared?'

To Mrs. Bird she said,

"I am sure it will be a delicious luncheon, Mrs. Bird. I will make out a list of what you will require for dinner tonight and Jacobs can ride to the village to fetch it."

Mrs. Bird did not reply and Ilina added,

"When he goes to the village, he must ask Gladys to come up to give you a hand. I am sure that His Grace can afford to pay her and perhaps we could ask her to help tomorrow until I have things straightened out."

As she spoke, she wondered if the Duke could afford Gladys or anybody else, but there was no use in worrying the Birds with this problem.

She was only praying that things would not prove to be as bad as she suspected and, if they were, what could she do about it?

*

Back in the study, her cheeks a little flushed from her haste, Ilina spoke to the Duke,

"Luncheon will be ready in a few minutes and I hope Your Grace will enjoy it. But I do warn you there is not a great deal to eat in the house, although I promise that things will be better by dinnertime."

The Duke looked at her and then asked,

"Are you intending to have luncheon with me, Miss Ashley?"

"No, of course not, Your Grace. I eat in my own room."

And then she added,

"I shall be ready to discuss matters after luncheon with Your Grace and will be waiting here if you need me."

She curtseyed and then went from the room while he was still finishing his glass of sherry.

As soon as the Duke was in the dining room, sitting at the head of the table in a high-backed carved chair that had been occupied by all the Dukes before him, Ilina helped in the background.

While Bird carried in the claret, she took the soup plate out of the oven and put it on a tray, found the silver spoon marked with the family crest and helped Mrs. Bird pour the soup into the large silver tureen.

When the omelette was ready and nicely browned on top, Ilina carried it and the vegetables to just outside the dining room door so that old Bird did not have to walk any further than was necessary.

He had been an excellent butler in his time and she knew that he would make no mistakes in serving the Duke or in keeping his glass filled. But his legs hurt him and if he had to walk about for long, he grew slower and slower.

Fortunately to go with the omelette there were plenty of new potatoes that she had dug up yesterday and a good portion of green peas.

Lastly Bird took in the cheese of which there was only a minute portion and Ilina heard him say,

"I'm afraid, Your Grace, we can't provide you with the sort of meal that Your Grace is accustomed to. Things have been difficult lately and we can only hope that now Your Grace's come home everything'll be very much better."

"They could hardly be worse, could they?" the Duke responded in an uncompromising tone.

"We've been hard put to make ends meet, Your Grace," Bird said, "and her Ladyship worried herself sick after His Grace died when she realised just how bad things were."

Listening, Ilina drew in her breath.

She had forgotten to tell Bird not to speak about her, but she knew that what he was saying was out of loyalty, as if he could not bear the new Duke to blame her for the shortcomings and poverty at The Abbey.

"I understand that Lady Ilina has gone North," the Duke remarked.

Again Ilina held her breath, wondering if she had told Bird what she was supposed to have done.

Then she could breathe again as he replied,

"I believe so, Your Grace."

Bird had obviously not yet found a bottle of port in the cellar and, when the Duke had finished his cheese, he drank another glass of claret before he rose from the table.

As he did so, Ilina sped quickly back to the study and was waiting demurely by the window when he entered.

She dropped him a small curtsey as she said,

"Do you wish to talk to me now, Your Grace, or would you rather rest?"

"I have not yet reached to the stage where I have to rest after luncheon," the Duke said sarcastically, "and I suggest, Miss Ashley, that you now tell me the whole dismal story from start to finish. I presume you have had your luncheon?"

"Yes, thank you."

She had eaten only a piece of the crust from the cottage loaf that Mrs. Bird had baked that morning while she was waiting for the Duke to finish the omelette.

She had surmised correctly that there would be nothing left over and there was hardly enough cheese for one person let alone two.

It also worried her that there was nothing for the Birds, unless there was a little cold rabbit left from yesterday, but she had the idea that this had gone into the soup.

'We cannot go on like this,' she reflected to herself.

She knew now that she had to tell the Duke the truth, however unpalatable it might be, and it was up to him to find a solution to the whole desperate situation.

Without waiting for him to suggest it, she sat down on a chair in front of the desk and began the story of how her grandfather had been very extravagant and had also left a mountain of debts when he died.

She went on to explain that her father had for the first years after inheriting lived on the interest that came from investments and the rents from the estate.

She told him how the farmers had been achieving good prices until the Government allowed cheap food to be brought into the country and there were several properties that had been let at quite high rents to people who also kept up the land when they were tenants.

Then the note in Ilina's voice made clear the unhappy state of affairs when gradually the tenants left and there was nobody to replace them.

The farms began to lose money and the Home Farm on which they had relied for their food became more and more ineffective.

Her father had not worried. He had gone on living as he wanted to, being Master of his own hunt, keeping a large number of horses and he and her mother going to London whenever it pleased them.

They would open the London house, enjoy a Season and attend several Court functions when her mother wore the family jewels.

At last her father had been aware that there was no more money for such a way of life and he had had to be more or less content to live in the country.

Then her mother had died unexpectedly, David had been killed and her father had the accident that had rendered him a cripple.

From that moment there had been nothing but despair and a poverty that grew worse month by month.

Only as she finished speaking, did Ilina realise that the Duke was listening to her attentively, his eyes on her face, and he had not spoken a single word since she began.

She felt suddenly shy while her voice trailed away into silence.

Still the Duke did not speak and she said almost desperately,

'That is what happened and, if I have described it somewhat dramatically, Your Grace must understand that as I was here and my father was so – close to the Duke – it all seemed as if it was – happening to me as well as to the Bury family."

"I suppose I should be grateful for your interest and your sympathy."

He did not, however, sound particularly grateful as he went on,

"And now, as you appear to have made it your problem as well as mine, Miss Ashley, I suggest you tell me what I can do about it."

Ilina drew in her breath.

"If, as I suspect, Your Grace has no money of your own to put things to rights, then as you cannot sell the house and I cannot believe that you wish it to fall to the ground, something has to be done!"

She paused and went on speaking rapidly,

"Although it may be very difficult for you, I feel that you will – save the house and the estate somehow."

"Why should you think that?"

She made a gesture with her hands.

"I don't know, but perhaps what is needed is a man in charge and someone who is – perhaps in many ways – ruthless."

"Is that necessary?"

"I think you will have to be ruthless if you are to preserve The Abbey."

She did not look at him as she was speaking, but she then said,

"If things have to be sold – perhaps some of them illegally because they are entailed – it would not be wrong if it meant that the – house could be saved."

The Duke looked at her for a moment.

Then he said,

"I am surprised at what you are suggesting, Miss Ashley!"

"Although it may seem – wrong and wicked – there is nothing else that can be done," Ilina said in an unhappy little voice. "There are two Van Dykes here that are valuable. There is another picture by – Holbein – which is so beautiful that it would be – heart-breaking to see it go, but it would fetch a big price."

The Duke was silent for a moment and then he quizzed her,

"Are you really proposing that I should sell these things, even if they are entailed?"

"I know it's wrong, but there are people who know about such matters, buyers working on behalf of rich American or collectors in Europe, who would buy them secretly – and no one would know. At least not until your son inherited."

"Do you think he would be pleased to discover that his father that had crooked him?"

Ilina started as he asked the question, knowing how often her father had said that both Roland Bury and his son were crooks.

"B-but what else – can you do?" she asked miserably. "The roof needs repairing and the rain water is – flooding into rooms on the top floor. Quite a number of the panes of glass need replacing in the State rooms and, unless the casements are painted soon, the windows will fall out."

The Duke did not speak and she went on,

"The chimneys have not been swept for years because we could not afford to have it done and in the kitchen, the scullery and the store rooms the plaster is falling off the walls and would fall into the food, if there was any!"

"You are certainly making out a good case for me to do what is an illegal and, as you admit, a dishonourable act," the Duke said dryly. "Now let me hear your suggestions, Miss Ashley, which I imagine are just as revolutionary, for the estate."

"I have thought and thought about what could be done," Ilina said, "and, although Mr. Wicker has suggested that there is quite a large amount of timber that can be cut down and sold, that would be only a drop in the ocean."

"Is that all?"

"There are the leaking cottages where the pensioners are housed," Ilina replied. "The alms houses, which have been abandoned, the orphanage which has existed for two hundred years, but there has been no money to pay a Master and Mistress and the school, which was always paid for by the reigning Duke, is needless to say closed."

She drew in her breath before she added,

"There are two Livings that Parsons have not been appointed to because it has always been the responsibility of the Duke of Tetbury to pay their stipends."

There was silence and then the Duke commented,

"It is certainly a very depressing tale. Frankly, Miss Ashley I had expected on my return, to find everything carrying on in the same way as it had in the past."

He hesitated for a moment and then went on to say,

"It is obvious I must decide what must be done before I return to where I have come from."

Ilina looked at him in astonishment.

"Are – are you – saying," she asked in a low voice, "that you do – not intend to live here?"

"Of course!" The Duke answered. "Why should I? I had no wish to be the Duke and I never suspected in my wildest dreams that I would inherit."

Ilina could find no answer to this and he went on,

"I have my own life and my own interests. I am quite happy, I can assure you, Miss Ashley, without encumbering myself with the trappings of aristocracy, which I consider very much out of date and a house and estate that have apparently already gone to rack and ruin."

He spoke harshly and Ilina clasped her hands together and said with a little cry of horror,

"Are you – telling me that you don't – care about the f-family – or everything that has mattered for three hundred years to the Burys?"

"Why should I?"

Because she was so deeply upset by what he was saying, Ilina rose from her chair to stand for a moment looking up at the second Duke in the picture over his head.

Then she walked to the window to stare out at the sunshine glinting on the lake and shining through the branches of the trees that were just beginning to bloom with the first buds of spring.

"How can it mean – nothing to you?" she asked in a low voice as if she spoke to herself. "You are a Bury and the blood of your ancestors runs in your veins. They have fought and died for England all down the centuries and for each of them the focal point of their lives has always been The Abbey."

She paused before she went on,

"Every owner has added his own individual style to it. There was Sir Wallace Bury who changed it after the Dissolution of the Monasteries into a private house and made it, as you will find in the history of the family, so delightful a place that Queen Elizabeth herself came from London to see it and stayed for three nights while he fêted her."

She was thinking as she carried on slowly,

"Later it became a refuge for the Royalists and numerous secret passages were built in it so that they could escape from the Roundheads. Lord Bury built a new wing, some of which still remains."

She did not look at the Duke, but she felt that he was listening as she said,

"After that every Bury added some lovely and perfect piece of it so that it has become in my opinion a house made of love. That is what it vibrates to everybody of their blood, so that they cannot fail to hear it call to them. Wherever they may wander over the world, The Abbey is always home."

When she finished speaking, Ilina felt the tears prick her eyes and because she was afraid that the Duke would see them and think it strange in somebody who was not of the same blood, she turned round and stood with her back to him.

She knew as she did so that, because he was surprised at what she had said, his eyes were boring their way into her back.

"You are certainly very eloquent, Miss Ashley," he observed at length, "and I suppose I should be touched that you should care so greatly for something that is not yours but mine."

She did not speak and after a moment he went on,

"To me The Abbey has always been a fortress that I was barred from and, as I expect you know, my father was ignored and ostracised first by the late Duke and then by the whole family."

"But he still talked about the house and told you what it was like," Ilina said softly.

She was remembering he had said that he expected there to be footmen in the hall as his father had told him there had always been.

The Duke then replied,

"I suppose, now I think of it, that my father did talk to me about it and he was very proud of his pedigree. What he deeply resented was the attitude of the family towards him."

"But you are not – your father!"

"I too was not accepted and not allowed to visit what you call our 'home' until now after thirty-four years when I find myself in possession of it."

"I do understand your bitterness," Ilina remarked, "but please, will you do something?"

"It depends what you are asking me to do."

"Will you try to look at The Abbey and all its problems without prejudice? Will you consider the house not as an encumbrance but as part of you? And remember that what it is asking you to give it is your heart and your mind."

She spoke pleadingly and the Duke said,

"You have greatly surprised me, Miss Ashley, by what you have said and there is no doubt that the house has captivated *you*! What will you feel when you have to leave?"

There was silence.

And then Ilina asked him,

"Are you – are you telling me you do not – wish me to stay here?"

"I am merely saying for the moment that I find your affection for my house somewhat touching and because you apparently have given it your heart, I can only agree to try to do what you have asked of me."

"You mean that? You really mean it?" Ilina asked eagerly.

"You have really given me no choice and, as you are apparently the only person who knows anything about the house, the estate, the accounts and, of course, the debts, we had better start at the very beginning."

"Where is that?" Ilina asked a little breathlessly.

The Duke smiled.

"I think a conducted tour of the house and its contents and, of course, a lecture on the talents, the achievements and the virtues of my illustrious forebears."

He was speaking mockingly, but there was not so much acidity or sarcasm in his voice as there had been before.

Ilina walked towards him.

"I would like to do that, Your Grace, I would like it very much. But please – will you promise me something?"

"What is that?"

"That you will not erect a barrier before we even start between the house – yourself and – the family."

There was a poignant pause before she went on,

"There are very few of them left. They no longer come here, but, if you cared about them, they would come back because they want to and, if they knew that you liked the house, you would mean so much to them."

"Now you are threatening me, Miss Ashley," the Duke protested.

CHAPTER THREE

Ilina rose very early as she always did and this morning it was more important than usual.

Yesterday, as they went round the house, the Duke had said very little while she explained which parts had been added by successive holders of the title and how the cloisters had remained incorporated each time the house had been altered.

Her stories were very entertaining about various eccentric Burys who had lived at The Abbey.

When at six o'clock she glanced at the clock, thinking that dinner would be in an hour's time, the Duke remarked,

"I imagine my servant has arrived by now."

"Servant?"

"I am sure you must have thought it strange that I arrived without any luggage," the Duke replied.

Ilina felt that he was rebuking her for what she now realised was an oversight on her part, simply because she had been so surprised to see him.

It had never entered her head that he would have a servant with him, although now she thought of it, her father, of course, had never travelled without his valet. She could remember when she was young and before they had become so poor how he and her mother went to London with a whole entourage of valets, lady's maids, secretaries, grooms, coachmen and extra footmen to augment the staff in the London house.

"I am sorry," she said humbly, "I cannot think how I could have forgotten that you came empty-handed."

As she thought of it, she hoped that the Duke's servant would not expect old Bird to carry up any trunks or cases and, as if he read her thoughts' the Duke said,

"Don't worry, Singh has looked after me for many years and is a very capable man."

When Ilina saw Singh, she was astonished because he was a Sikh and with his white turban and dark beard he looked very strange in The Abbey.

Equally he was a strong, handsome man and she was to realise from the very beginning how competent he was.

She had, before she went round the house with the Duke, told Mrs. Bird to take the best sheets, which were monogrammed and trimmed with lace, out of the linen cupboard and put them in the Master bedroom, which her father had always used.

She had intended while the Duke had dinner to make up the bed for him and, when they came from the library, which had been the last place they visited, the Duke's servant was waiting for him in the hall.

He salaamed in Eastern fashion as the Duke said,

"Oh, here you are, Singh. You have brought everything that I wanted with you?"

"Yes, Master," Singh replied in very good English. "Some tradesmen kept me waiting longer than promised, but I have most things the Lord Sahib requires."

"Good," the Duke said, "and I imagine you found my room?"

"Yes, Lord Sahib and have made up bed."

He looked a little curiously at Ilina and the Duke said,

"This is Miss Ashley, who is in charge of the house. If there is anything you need, you should ask her assistance."

Singh then salaamed to Ilina and she told him,

"I am sure that the butler will show you where you can sleep and will make you as comfortable as possible."

"Thank you, Memsahib."

Singh salaamed again, and the Duke turned to Ilina,

"As Singh will have my bath ready, I will go now and change for dinner. I shall expect you to dine with me. Miss Ashley."

Ilina hesitated, wondering what she should reply and he said with a slight twist to his lips,

"I find that the ghosts of my ancestors and the disapproving way that they look down at me from their frames somewhat overwhelming and definitely indigestible. The least you can do is to go on trying to persuade me that they are different from how they appear."

The way he spoke made Ilina give a little laugh as she replied,

"Thank you, Your Grace, for your invitation. I am sure that you are aware it is not usual for the Curator to eat in the dining room."

"If you are worried about the conventions, Miss Ashley," the Duke commented dryly, "I cannot imagine who you are afraid of shocking except, of course, those who are no longer with us thank goodness!"

The way he spoke took the smile from Ilina's lips.

Then, as he walked slowly up the fine carved Georgian staircase, she ran to the pantry.

"His Grace insists that I dine with him," she told Bird, who was taking the silver candelabrum from the safe.

"That's as it should be, my Lady."

"Miss!" Ilina corrected him. "Lay another place and, as Mrs. Bird will have Gladys to help her, she will not miss me."

She did not wait for old Bird to reply, but ran up a side staircase that led her to the West wing where the schoolroom was situated.

When it came to dinner gowns, she had very little choice except for those that had belonged to her mother and were hanging in the wardrobe of the room that had once been occupied by the Governess.

Until now Ilina had never had an occasion to wear them and so she had not had time to change them from a crinoline into a bustle.

But, rather than wear the old gown that she had put on every evening while her father was ill and there had been nobody to see her and which she thought was almost bursting at the seams, she took down one of her mother's pretty dresses.

It was made in the blue that matched her eyes and the crinoline swung out from her slender waist while her shoulders were encircled with a bertha of lace embroidered with small pearls.

When she had it on, she wondered if the Duke would think that she looked like a picture in the family album and almost ludicrously out of fashion.

Then she told herself that it did not worry her what he thought. What was important was to persuade him to repair the house and the farms.

She could not believe that he had been serious when he said that he had no interest in being a Duke.

But she had the alarming feeling that there was nobody but herself to persuade him that he must not only do his duty but bring honour to the family name and make it as prestigious as it had been in the past.

Because she was frightened that she might fail, she looked up at the portrait of her brother and said in her heart,

'Help me, David. Help me to make him see, as you did, that however remiss Papa may have been and, although Grandpapa's extravagances have crippled us, the Burys must still contribute to the greatness of England, just as you would have done if you had lived.'

As she spoke, she thought that David's eyes were twinkling at her as if he understood, and at the same time was almost laughing at her intensity.

It was as if he told her that eventually the Duke would become conscious of what was required of him simply because of the blood that coursed in his veins and the house itself would speak more eloquently than she could.

'I only hope you are right,' she said as if he had argued with her. 'But he is a strange man and I don't like him."

'You wanted him to be ruthless,' she thought David said to her and she replied,

'But *for* us – not against.'

Then, as if she was suddenly aware that there was no more time to go on talking to her brother unless she was to be late for dinner, she ran downstairs to find, as she expected, that the Duke was already in the study.

He held a glass in his hand and one quick glance told Ilina that there were two decanters on the silver tray that stood on the grog table, which meant that Bird had located the Madeira as she had told him to do.

Then she realised that the Duke was looking at her somewhat critically and, although she had had no intention of making any explanation, she said almost despite herself,

"I am afraid you will think I look very old-fashioned, but in this part of the world we have only just realised that the crinoline is out of date and that the bustle has taken its place."

"You look very charming. Miss Ashley."

He spoke in his usual dry, almost sarcastic tone, and she did not feel that it was much of a compliment.

When he offered it, she accepted a small glass of Madeira, thinking that it was something she had not drunk since her father was crippled and the doctor had forbidden him any form of alcohol in case it should increase the pain that he was already suffering.

Sometimes he would demand that a bottle of brandy be brought upstairs and he would drink it to drown the pain.

When she remonstrated with him, he shouted furiously that, if he wanted to kill himself, he would do so without asking her permission.

He could be very rude and very aggressive and, as the months went by and nothing the doctor gave him was of any use, Ilina felt it was only right that he should have what he wanted.

If alcohol helped him, why should she object?

When all the brandy in the cellar was finished, and there had been a great deal of it, her father had drunk what other spirits there were and was demanding more, which they could not possibly afford, when he died.

Because the way he behaved when he was drunk was to Ilina's mind so humiliating that her father's valet had refused sometimes to let her enter his bedroom.

Towards the end she was saved from seeing him except the next morning when he was suffering from a hangover.

This made him so disagreeable that he was hardly recognisable as the man she had known as a child and whom she had loved.

She often wondered how her mother would have coped with such a situation.

Then she told herself miserably that, because her father had loved her mother, he would never in her lifetime have sunk to such depths of depravity.

On the other hand she only made him worse because he hated her for not being the son he wanted her to be.

Now it was all over and she tried never to think about it.

But now there was a new problem of the new Duke to confront her.

As he drank a small glass of sherry slowly and she thought abstemiously, Singh came to the door of the study to announce,

"Dinner is served, Master."

Ilina was glad that old Bird did not have to walk the long way from the dining room to the study, which would have been a tax on his legs.

She was even gladder when they reached the dining room to find that Singh was also waiting at table and, she noticed, fetching the dishes from the kitchen.

Tonight's meal was very different from what the Duke had been given for luncheon and Ilina guessed that he must have given the Birds some money to purchase it.

There was soup to start with, but now it was made of cream and fresh mushrooms, which Jacobs must have been able to buy in the village.

To follow there was a leg of spring lamb, which Ilina found delicious having subsisted for weeks on rabbits that Jacobs snared in the shrubs near the house or on pigeons, which the farmers gave her when they were scaring them off the crops.

Mrs. Bird had cooked the lamb perfectly and the young chicken that followed it was so tender that it seemed to melt in the mouth.

The Duke did full justice to both courses and appeared to enjoy the gooseberry fool and the stuffed tomatoes that followed as a savoury.

It was the sort of meal that her father had appreciated when her mother was alive and Ilina knew that Mrs. Bird cooked well, especially when she had Gladys to whom she could demonstrate her culinary skill.

To her surprise the Duke said as he had a second helping of the lamb,

"There is no excuse, seeing how good your cook is, for you to be so thin, Miss Ashley. Or are you one of those tiresome females who are afraid of putting on weight?"

Ilina laughed, knowing how little opportunity she had of being anything but a skeleton seeing how short of food they had been.

Sometimes when the chickens refused to lay and Jacob's snares caught no rabbits, there was nothing but vegetables from the overgrown garden to eat.

She had often thought that if it was not for the potatoes, which because Williams's arthritis was so bad she herself had planted, they would all have starved.

In which case when the Duke had come to inspect his inheritance, he would have found the house peopled with skeletons.

"What is worrying you?" the Duke asked suddenly.

"Do I look – worried?"

"You have looked worried ever since we met," he replied. "Is it because I don't agree with you on the inestimable importance of my ancestors?"

"Surely what I have said makes you realise your own importance?" Ilina said, anxious to get away from the subject of herself.

The Duke laughed.

"I doubt if living here would make me feel important. Certainly not as things are at the moment."

"Once you have established yourself and people realise that there is another Duke of Tetbury, then there are a great number of opportunities open to you that you would not have anywhere else."

"And what can they be?" the Duke asked sceptically.

He leaned back in the high armchair as he spoke and she had to admit that even though the evening clothes he wore were shabby and somewhat unconventional he had a presence that was inescapable.

She could not quite explain it to herself, but she was conscious of his vitality and a strength that was not entirely physical but seemed to emanate from him.

She found it overpowering in some ways and admirable in others.

'It is what a Duke should be,' she thought and remembered that it was what her father had been like when he was a young man.

She also thought that this particular strength, or was it a vibration, must have come from all her ancestors and especially from the second Duke, who had been a hero in India and in consequence received the gift of the Nizam's jewels.

Then she told herself that she hated the present Duke because he had no feeling as he should have for the family, the house or anything else that she had shown him.

Because she was so eager for him to be impressed, she hardly realised at the time that he had said nothing as she showed him the pictures, the *Sèvres* china that one Duke had brought from France and the armoury where from early in their history the Burys had begun to assemble weapons of every sort.

It had now become a unique collection, as were the cups, the boxes and the objects of every sort and kind that had been presented to them in different parts of the world.

There was also one room that had cabinets containing the medals that various Burys had won on the battlefields or been awarded by the reigning Monarch.

Among these was the Order of the Garter glittering with diamonds and only one stone from it, Ilina had often thought, would keep them in food for a least six months.

Then there were foreign Orders, which were decorated with real jewels and which were so pretty that her mother had often said laughingly that she would like to wear one round her neck.

The Duke had hardly spoken a word and now, looking at him sitting at the end of the table and wearing a cynical expression on his face, Ilina thought despairingly that to him the house only contained relics of the past that he was not even remotely interested in.

"Tomorrow," the Duke said as Bird poured him out another glass of claret, "I would like to see the estate and, of course, the farms that you have described to me."

There was a little silence.

Then Ilina said,

"You realise that you have to ride?"

"Of course," the Duke answered. "I presume you have a horse for me?"

"Actually you have two to choose from," Ilina answered. "They are in the stables in which the fourth Duke kept forty horses, but one of them belongs to me."

She thought that the Duke looked surprised and she added quickly,

"I brought Pegasus – with me when I – came here."

He made no comment and she went on,

"The other horse I bought cheaply or rather Mr. Wicker did on behalf of the estate a year ago."

The Duke raised his eyebrows and she continued,

"It was a young horse that a local farmer found too obstreperous and too wild to manage. I have therefore broken him in with the help of Jacobs and he is not quite amenable unless he is upset."

She paused and looked at the Duke a little uncomfortably as she said,

"I expect you are a good rider and I am quite prepared to lend you Pegasus, if that is what you prefer."

"I think you are insulting me, Miss Ashley."

"No, please, I don't mean to," Ilina said quickly. "It is just that I thought perhaps you would be more used to riding on – elephants and camels than on horses."

"Yaks, dromedaries and buffalo," the Duke added. "Of course, Miss Ashley, you show the usual ignorance of the insular English with regard to foreign countries."

Ilina made an apologetic little sound and he carried on,

"I assure you in Calcutta we have just as good racehorses as you will see as Ascot or Epsom and I am not afraid of your wild horse."

Because he spoke so scathingly, Ilina could only say humbly,

"I am – sorry and, of course, I am very – ignorant of the life you have – lived before you came here."

The idea that any man dressed as badly as he was made her want to add that she could not expect him to have a stable of racehorses.

But she knew that it would be rude and she only said as if in her own defence,

"I will tell Jacobs that we will require the horses tomorrow morning and I was only thinking of which one he must put on the side-saddle."

"I know exactly what you were thinking, Miss Ashley," the Duke said sharply, "and, as I am quite certain that all my ancestors were exceptionally fearless riders, I am confident that I shall not prove the exception to the rule."

Ilina gave a little sigh, thinking that she had made a mess of what seemed to her quite a reasonable question.

Then, as if he felt that he had been unnecessarily harsh, the Duke suggested,

"Tell me about yourself. It seems strange that your relatives should allow you to live alone in this house and to work yourself to the bone, however much you may be paid for doing so."

He paused and then he added,

"Incidentally, what is your salary?"

Because Ilina had not expected him to ask the question so quickly, she had to think swiftly before she replied,

"I am supposed to receive forty pounds a year, Your Grace, for my services as Librarian and Curator, but I have, as it happens, received no wages for quite some time."

"That does not surprise me," the Duke remarked. "It seems extraordinary that you have not looked for employment elsewhere."

"I am very happy here and, as I told you, I have always lived on the estate."

"And you would be afraid to go elsewhere?"

"Very afraid – in fact I – want to stay here. Please – let me stay."

She was pleading with him and there was an undoubted expression of fear in her eyes that he did not miss.

"We must talk about that another time," he answered, "but I still find it strange that you prefer this lonely life in an empty house to being with young people of your own age and, of course, young men to pay you compliments."

Ilina laughed.

"That is the last thing I want and I am not entirely alone."

"No? You have a friend?"

"Somebody who matters to me more than anything else in the world," Ilina replied, "who is always glad to see me, is never critical and who I know loves me."

There was no mistaking the surprise on the Duke's face or the mocking note in his voice as he asked,

"Who is this paragon? And am I to assume from what you have just said that you are about to be married?"

Ilina shook her head thinking it amusing to puzzle him.

"No," she replied, "Although I promise you, that if the Gods were kind enough to turn him into a Centaur, that is exactly what I should be ready to do."

Far quicker than she expected the Duke came the point of what she was saying and replied,

"Now I understand that you are referring to your horse."

"Yes, Pegasus," Ilina smiled. "Although you may not believe it, when I am riding him, as I do every morning, I do not miss anybody or anything else."

"Then you must be very different from most young women of your age."

"Have you known many?" Ilina asked him.

She remembered that David had said that most of his friends found girls dull and preferred to date and flirt with married women.

The Duke twisted his lips as he replied,

"Every year more and more young English women come to India in search of husbands. They are known as the 'Fishing Fleet' and I assure you I make quite certain that I am not involved with them."

"Why not?" Ilina asked. "Do they frighten you?"

The Duke laughed.

"No, but I have no wish to be married. He travels fastest who travels alone and I am very content to be a bachelor."

Ilina was silent for a moment and then she said,

"One day there will have to be a seventh Duke of Tetbury."

"Once again you are pointing out to me my duty. Miss Ashley. It is a word I dislike so I think I should tell you that I have no intention of marrying. As far as I am concerned, there will be no seventh Duke, or if there is, he will not be my son!"

Ilina gave a little cry of horror.

"But you cannot say that. I have not had time to tell you that after you there is no relative to inherit the title and it would in fact die out."

"Would that be such a catastrophe?"

"Of course it would. How can you possibly allow a family to die that has contributed so much to the history of this country?"

"However eloquent you may be, Miss Ashley," the Duke replied, "I cannot see that the last Duke contributed very much and his father merely incurred a mountain of debts, which is hardly something to evoke congratulations."

"He owned some very fine horses that won a number of the Classic races. He also collected the sporting pictures that hang in the Picture Gallery and which are unique."

"And, I understand, did not pay for a number of them!"

Because she knew that the Duke was jeering at her, Ilina felt her hatred of him rising with her anger and there seemed to be a little spark of fire in her eyes as she said,

"It is very easy to defame people who are dead. At the same time Your Grace has not yet told me in what way you have contributed to the country where you have been living. It is something I am anxious to hear."

There was a note in her voice that the Duke could not misunderstand and after a moment he said,

"As dinner is finished, Miss Ashley, and you are such a stickler for what is traditional, I think it would be correct for you to leave me to my port."

As she was well aware that he was striking back at her, Ilina felt the colour come into her cheeks and she rose from her chair and started to walk towards the door.

The Duke reached it first and opened it with a flourish.

She did not let him see how humiliated she felt, but lifted her chin as she stopped for a moment to say,

"Will you require me anymore this evening, Your Grace, or my I retire?"

"If that is what you would prefer, Miss Ashley, I understand," the Duke answered. "Undoubtedly it has been a long day for you and we are to ride before breakfast, which is the time I prefer. Shall we say seven o'clock?"

"I will be ready, Your Grace."

Ilina curtseyed and he bowed she thought mockingly as she swept through the door.

'I hate him!' she said to herself as she ran up the grand staircase and along the passage that led to her rooms in the West wing.

Only when she had closed the door behind her did she go to stand in front of David's picture and say to him,

'Now what do you think of the new Duke? I have failed – utterly and completely failed to reach him!'

She stared up at her brother's face and added,

'Oh, David, how could you have been killed when you should have been here? Somehow we would have managed to keep the house going and the estate, because we love it.'

She felt the tears come into her eyes as she went on,

'Papa was right about Cousin Roland and Sheridan must be like him in every way, spoilt, selfish and detestable! I hate him. *I hate him* and nothing I can say to him will make any difference.'

Because she not only hated the Duke but felt that she herself had failed the family in not convincing him how much his inheritance mattered, the tears ran down her cheeks.

When she finally climbed into bed, she cried herself to sleep.

*

Nevertheless, although there were lines under her eyes that had not been there the day before, when Ilina went to the stables, she felt the inevitable lift of her heart at the thought that she would see Pegasus.

However black everything else might be, she loved him and he loved her.

He heard her coming and was at the door of his stall as she entered it and put her arms round his neck.

"Oh, darling," she whispered, "whatever happens, I will never lose you. Even if we have to leave here and beg in the streets, we will still be together."

She laid her cheek against the horse's neck and her eyes were closed with the intensity of her feelings so that she started when a voice came from behind her,

"You are very demonstrative to your horse, Miss Ashley, and I hope Pegasus appreciates the sacrifices you are prepared to make for him, as the Burys have apparently omitted to do for you."

Slowly Ilina took her arms from Pegasus's neck.

As he nuzzled his nose against her as if asking for more of her attention, she turned her head to see the Duke at the open door of the stall looking, she thought, more cynical than usual.

"Your Grace is early," she remarked, in what she hoped was a calm cold voice, but which actually sounded breathless and shy.

"It is a habit that comes from having lived in the East for so long," the Duke replied. "And now I am waiting for you to show me the animal that you are hoping will unseat and throw me."

"I am hoping nothing of the sort!" Ilina retorted.

Jacobs came into the stable at that moment saying as he did so,

"Good mornin', m – miss. You're earlier than usual. I were just about to put a saddle on Rufus."

"His Grace is waiting to ride him, Jacobs."

Turning to the Duke she said,

"This is Jacobs. He has been here for thirty-five years and was hoping that Your Grace would fill the empty stalls as they were in the past."

She thought that such a statement might embarrass him, but, as he glanced at her, she was aware that he knew what she was attempting to do and was merely amused.

He shook hands with Jacobs and spoke to him pleasantly without being in the least condescending and she realised to her surprise that Jacobs liked him.

Jacobs had a way with horses that Ilina often thought was different from that of anybody else. She knew too that, just as he could judge a good horse as soon as he saw it, he was also a judge of men.

As he hurried to put the saddle on Rufus, he was talking to the Duke as one lover of horseflesh to another and it was a language that only they could understand.

When finally they rode out of the stables, Ilina was aware that she need not have doubted the Duke's ability as a rider.

He seemed to be part of the horse just as her father had been and she knew that it was an ability, whether he liked it or not, that he had inherited from his ancestors, who had all been great horsemen.

Because Pegasus was fresh and Rufus was trying to play up his new rider, they galloped across the Park, Ilina leading along a path that was free from rabbit holes and fallen branches of trees.

When finally they were out on flat land that led to the Home Farm and which should by now have been ploughed and sown, she knew without the Duke saying anything that he realised it was neglected.

Because she was quite certain that the Hendersons, who lived at the Home Farm, would never remember that she was supposed to be 'Miss Ashley', Ilina insisted on the Duke visiting them alone while she rode Pegasus round the fields until he could rejoin her.

Without anything being said she was quite aware that he must have seen the condition of the farmhouse, the barns with their roofs blown off and the empty cow stalls which, like everything else, were in urgent need of repair.

They rode in silence to the next farm, which had once been let for quite a good rent, but was now empty and desolate.

The Duke looked at it without comment and they rode on again until, feeling that he must have seen enough, Ilina suggested that they should return for breakfast.

As they reached the stables, where Jacobs was waiting for them, the Duke said,

"Thank you, Miss Ashley. You have certainly not exaggerated the poor condition of the estate I have inherited and the fact that nothing has been cultivated on what was considered in the past to be good land."

His voice was scathing as he finished,

"I can only imagine that this neglect should be ascribed to the Duke's long illness or should the blame be on those who were supposed to be looking after the estate?"

Ilina thought that he was accusing Mr. Wicker of incompetence and replied quickly,

"There is no one to blame except the Duke who was a helpless cripple when he died. His Solicitors always urged caution and economy, but he would not listen to them – until it was too late!"

"It's not surprising," the Duke said. "At the same time he had the impertinence to accuse my father of a great many crimes he did not commit."

Since there was nothing Ilina could say to this, she simply dismounted and hurried away from the stables, leaving him with Jacobs.

When she went to the breakfast room, she found that Singh and Bird together had been arranging everything just as it had been when she was a child.

There were three silver dishes with lighted candles underneath them to keep them hot and there was a new cottage loaf of freshly baked bread, as well as a big silver rack filled with golden slices of toast.

Because it was so different from anything that she had seen for years, Ilina, despite what the Duke had said to her, felt her heart leaping.

She even smiled at him as he came into the room and pretended not to notice what she thought was a stormy expression on his face.

She had already helped herself from one of the dishes and she thought that he must be hungry as he sat down at the table with a well-filled plate.

They ate for a little while in silence.

Then as Ilina asked him if he would like some more coffee and filled his cup he said,

"I suppose I had better see the rest of the horrors this morning."

"It is for you to decide, Your Grace."

"Very well, let's get it over."

As soon as they were on their horses again, Ilina took him to the village. She showed him the row of cottages where the pensioners lived and there was no need to itemise what needed doing.

The alms-houses, as she had already told him, were closed, with panes of glass in every window broken.

Ilina then went to one of the furthest farms where the dwelling house had once been a delightful red stone Manor.

The windows were boarded up, the garden was a wilderness, the building behind it was roofless and the land a mass of weeds.

"The last tenant," she said, "wanted to buy the house and five hundred acres at a knock-down price. When he found it impossible to do so, he went elsewhere. No one else has been interested in 'renting' it as nothing could be repaired."

The Duke was silent and rode on.

There were two more farms for him to inspect, one had a couple nearly as old as the Hendersons with one idiot son to help them. The other was empty.

As they arrived back at The Abbey and left the horses in the stables, the Duke said,

"I want to talk to you, but I imagine you would like first to change. So perhaps you would come to my study in an hour's time."

The way he spoke made Ilina glance at him apprehensively, but she merely replied,

"You sound very like a schoolteacher who is going to find fault with me, but I will not keep Your Grace waiting."

She walked into the hall and up the stairs without looking back.

When she looked at the worn riding habit that she had taken off, she felt it made the Duke as contemptuous of her as he was of the dilapidation of the house, the farms and the land.

She wondered, as he had spoken in such a solemn way, what he had to say to her.

It was not until she was dressed in the same green gown that she had worn the day before that she glanced up at her brother's picture and asked herself whether the Duke was going to agree with her suggestion of selling some of the pictures surreptitiously.

She might hate him, but she had the feeling, although she could not account for it, that despite all her father had said he would not do anything he knew to be dishonourable.

'If only David was here,' she thought, 'he would agree that it would be better to sacrifice some pictures than The

Abbey and, if it is a choice between the two, The Abbey must come first.'

She hurried downstairs to find the Duke who was, as she had expected, already seated at the desk in the study.

He was making notes on a piece of paper in front of him. He looked up as she entered the room and, as she walked towards him, watched her with what she thought was an enigmatic expression on his face.

Then, as she reached the desk, he said,

"Now, Cousin Ilina suppose we stop playing games and get down to business?"

Ilina stood very still and the colour rose in her cheeks.

For a moment she thought that she would contradict what he had said and declare that she was in fact who she pretended to be.

Then she told herself that she would not stoop to lying any further and she must accept that he was more perceptive than she had imagined him to be.

"H-how do you know who – I am?"

"I am not completely half-witted," the Duke replied, "and, as the servants have stumbled and stuttered over your name every time they speak to you, it was not difficult to suspect that there was something wrong. Actually there is a picture of you in the Duchess's Drawing Room too."

Ilina smiled.

"That is a picture of Mama when she married."

"You are very like her," the Duke commented dryly.

"I am sorry that I tried to deceive you," Ilina said, "but I thought it would perhaps be embarrassing that you should find me here and feel that I was an encumbrance on top of everything else."

"Is that what you are?"

"I-I am afraid so. You see, I have no money and really nowhere else to – go."

"And of course, you have not found the Nizam's jewels."

Ilina raised her eyebrows.

"You know that is what Papa left me in his will?"

"The Solicitors sent me a copy of the will when they wrote to tell me that your father had died."

"Since the jewels have been hidden since 1805 and are unlikely ever to be found, you can will understand the – predicament that I find – myself in."

"That is something I find worrying."

"Please don't worry on my account," Ilina said. "It is The Abbey and the estate that should concern you, as it concerns me."

Because she felt almost weak from learning that he had unmasked her so easily that she must have played her part very badly, she sat down on the chair in front of the desk.

Then her eyes were very wide and questioningly she asked,

"What are you – going to do? Not about – me but about – everything else?"

"That is what I want to talk to you about. I have tried, and I think honestly, to do as you asked me and look at everything without prejudice."

"And you have – come to some conclusion?"

The Duke nodded and it seemed to Ilina as if she held her breath.

Then she asked in a voice that was hardly audible,

"What have you – decided to do?"

"I have decided first," the Duke replied, "to return to where I belong and to the life I have become accustomed to."

Ilina stiffened.

Then she gave a little cry and it was almost like that of an animal caught in a trap.

"I cannot believe it! What about The Abbey, the estate and your – position here?"

"I am not interested in my position here," the Duke replied, "and in the future I shall not use my title."

Ilina was incapable of speech and he went on,

"Nor do I think that what you have shown me is worth the fortune that must be spent to restore and preserve it."

He finished speaking and Ilina, who had turned very pale, was aware that her hands were trembling as she asked,

"How can you do this? How can you – abdicate from everything that is – yours and to which, whether you like it or not – you belong?"

"I am nothing of the sort!" the Duke objected. "My father was never part of the family because they would not have him. He was made a scapegoat and treated as a 'black sheep'."

"That was a – long time ago."

"Not for me. I was brought up with my father's bitterness and resentment and with a burning sense of injustice at the way he was treated."

He laughed and it was not a very pleasant sound.

"I made up my mind when I was quite a small boy that one day I would avenge my father, whom I loved and admired, and now my opportunity has come. In fact if I did as I intended when I came here, I would burn the house down with my own hands!"

Ilina gave an exclamation of sheer horror as the Duke went on,

"Instead I will close it, box up the windows and leave it to rot. Our ancestors, Ilina, can feel in the future as isolated as my father felt and as I have felt too all my life until now."

"P-please – " Ilina began to say, but he interrupted her to go on,

"They can stare down from their frames at nobody and at nothing! They will remain here in an empty house that will be their tomb more effectively than the stones that cover their graves. That is my revenge for the way they treated my father and it will give me great pleasure to think of it."

There was silence and there was a sneering smile on the Duke lips, which told Ilina that he was waiting for her to protest and plead with him knowing that he would refuse to listen.

Then she said very quietly, as if she spoke from a long distance,

"And when you have the – satisfaction of knowing that you have – destroyed something beautiful, historic and – magnificent which for the moment is – yours and yours alone, will you then be – happy?"

"I shall know that what I have done is poetic justice!"

"For you – alone," Ilina whispered.

"For me and what is left of the family."

"For me will be only the – darkness and – misery of knowing that I have failed."

"What do you mean *failed*?" the Duke questioned.

Ilina was silent for a moment.

And then she said,

"When you came here yesterday, I hated you first because you had been so long in responding to my invitation and secondly because you were so indifferent –
"

"You hated me?" the Duke interrupted.

"I have come to hate you more and more every minute since you have been here," Ilina said quietly, "because I knew that everything that meant so much to the – family and which has survived for – three hundred years meant – nothing to you."

She turned and raised her head to look at the portrait of the second Duke as she went on,

"I did not however – imagine that you could think of anything so – wicked as to renounce your whole responsibility and abandon it – as you intend to do."

Her voice faltered but she carried on,

"I must have known instinctively that it was at the – back of your mind. That is why I hated you, as I hate you now! And, if there are any Burys left, they and their children and their children's children will – curse you."

She rose as she spoke and walked towards the window to stand with her back to him fighting against the tears that threatened to blind her eyes.

Then she heard him say in a rather different tone of voice,

"But, of course, Ilina, I still have to consider the problem of what to do with you."

She turned round.

"If you are offering me charity, Cousin Sheridan, don't waste your breath! I would rather starve or die than accept anything from you. You may throw me out of the house, but I will sleep in the woods or under a hayrick – and stay here."

Her voice broke, but she continued fiercely,

"Although you may think I am insane and that I am letting my – imagination run away with me, I know that those who have lived here in the past and my – brother David, who – should have been – here in your place, will help me."

She drew herself up so that she seemed immeasurably taller than she really was, as she then said very slowly,

"I shall somehow save The Abbey from decay and whatever you may do – however wicked your intentions towards it – I know in my heart that one day – another and better Bury than you will live here and he will be – worthy of our name!"

As Ilina finished speaking, she walked across the room, opened the door and went out, closing it almost unnaturally quietly behind her.

CHAPTER FOUR

When Ilina left the study, the Duke sat back in his chair and stared at the portraits of the two Dukes that he could see on the walls in front of him.

He was thinking that at last he had been able to say what had been on his mind ever since he could remember.

He had always imagined that, when he did tell the Burys exactly what he thought of them, there would be a much larger audience then one young girl who had stared at him with a stricken expression in her eyes.

When he was a small boy he had longed to see the family house that had appeared to be always on his father's lips, but whenever it was mentioned it brought a look of pain to his mother's face.

One day when he was about eight he had said to his father,

"I want to see Tetbury Abbey, Papa. Can we go over there? How far is it?"

His father had been silent for a moment before he had replied,

"It's a place you may never see, Sheridan, but if you do, spit on it on my behalf!"

It was some years later, he thought looking back, that he had begun to understand how bitterly his father resented the way that he had been treated by the fifth Duke, who was a cousin several times removed.

It was his mother who had told him that the two men, who were about the same age, had been at Eton together and their dislike of one another had started there mostly on the side of Lionel Bury, as he then was, who was jealous.

Roland Bury was a difficult man, but a great sportsman and when there was the question of either him or his cousin Lionel being picked for the First Eleven at cricket and he had been chosen, the animosity between him and Lionel had become almost violent.

The choice of his cousin had been such a blow to Lionel that from that moment he had never spoken to him again while they were at school.

When they grew up, there was a kind of armed truce between them and Roland Bury had attended one or two family gatherings at The Abbey being aware that the Duke looked at him with the same dislike as he had when they were at school.

Then another incident had made their feud as fiery and as vitriolic as it had been at Eton.

This time it was when Lionel had accused his cousin of bumping and boring in a steeplechase.

It was subsequently proved that his accusations were quite unjustified, but by that time the two men had been so excessively rude to each other that there was no chance of a reconciliation.

In fact the Duke unjustly called Roland a blackguard and a crook and informed him through his Solicitors that, if he attempted at any time to enter The Abbey, he would be thrown out by the servants.

Roland Bury had considered bringing a lawsuit against his cousin for slander, but his wife persuaded him that such an action would bring discredit on the family name, adding that she was sure that time was a great healer.

It was, as far as the two cousins were concerned, nothing of the sort and the Duke continued to decry Roland on every possible occasion.

To make things worse he informed him again through his Solicitors that not only was he barred from entering The Abbey but so was his son and any other member of his household.

His choice of words was so rude that Roland was again only restrained by his wife from bringing a case against him, but his bitterness and resentment was something that could not be hidden from his son.

Because Sheridan was aware that his father, whom he loved, was suffering, he hated his relatives who could be so unjust and on no good grounds.

Because the Burys had been a closely knit family under the previous Duke and The Abbey had always been open to any of them at any time, Roland received a great deal of sympathy from his other relatives.

Also since the Duke was a quarrelsome man, many of them too were soon at loggerheads with him and had their own grievances to air.

It was not surprising therefore that Sheridan grew up feeling that the Head of the Family was an ogre whose wickedness reflected on those who should have been depending on him for leadership and help.

As the years passed, while the Duke became impoverished, Roland Bury found himself, if not really poor, definitely in the position where he had to count what he spent and make economies in his way of living.

It was then that his son decided that, if he could not live in England in the style he would have wished, owning like his father, the best racehorses and enjoying the gaieties of London, he would go abroad.

He went off in an exploratory manner at first, undecided as to what he should do or how he should do it, thinking that somehow he would prove that he at any rate could manage without the Bury family and when the time came could confront them on equal terms.

He was well aware that, while his father and the rest of the older generation railed against the Duke, they were still because it was ingrained in them, rather like sheep without a shepherd.

Ever since they were children The Abbey had been the focal point where they all gravitated to automatically because it was part of their blood.

In the new world that Sheridan found in the East no one was particularly interested in Dukes and it was not thought degrading for a man born a gentleman to work.

Because he was exceedingly intelligent, he soon realised that what was needed where he was now living was organising ability and leadership.

He therefore set himself out to make a fortune and at the same time, although it seemed ridiculous, if he attained his goal, to achieve the possibility of avenging himself on the man who had made his father so unhappy.

"Why does The Abbey matter so much to Papa?" he had asked his mother one evening at dinner when Roland Bury had proclaimed furiously against the treachery of the Duke.

"It is difficult to make you understand, since you have never been there, how beautiful The Abbey is," his mother had replied. "And it is a monument to the achievements and the heroism of a family that has held it for over three hundred years."

She saw that her son was listening and had continued,

"When I first married your father, I found it impossible to understand why they should be so proud and in a way so conceited about themselves."

She gave a little laugh.

"It took me a long time to realise that it was not a personal conceit but a pride in their ancestors which made them genuinely believe in their hearts that the Burys were finer people than anybody else."

"Is that true, Mama?"

"It is something your father, I think, would not admit," his mother had answered, "but I know, because I love him, that it is what he believes. You can understand therefore how deeply he feels being cut off from The Abbey."

She paused as if trying to put her thoughts into order and then went on,

"In the past the Head of the Family always led them as if he was a General being followed onto the battlefield by the soldiers of his own Regiment."

"So it was the Burys against the world?"

"Exactly," his mother had replied. "And they were quite confident that they were invincible."

"Papa is very important here," Sheridan reasoned.

"But not as important as the Duke and our house, although it is very charming, can never hope to rival The Abbey."

There was no answer to this and Sheridan would lie awake sometimes in the heat of India or Siam and find himself thinking of the many tales that his father had told him about The Abbey.

He would imagine that he was bathing in the cool lake, lying in the shadow of a great tree in the Park, riding over the meadowland or, when it was snowing, finding the white world round The Abbey a complete enchantment.

He also remembered his father talking about shooting round the woods and watching the partridges rise out of the stubble.

He wondered if it was more enjoyable, just because it was at The Abbey, than shooting a tiger or stalking some elusive chamois in the rocky heights of the Himalayas.

The Abbey! Always The Abbey.

Inevitably his thoughts would come back to the Duke, who had barred his father from the Garden of Eden that he was by birth entitled to.

Now, he told himself, he would have his revenge.

The house would be boarded up with its treasures inside it and gradually the rats and mice would gnaw their way into the great State rooms and make their nests in the sofas and chairs.

Cobwebs would festoon the crystal chandeliers and the carved gold pelmets that had been specially designed for each room.

Dust would cover the floors and the great beds and, as the years passed, the pictures of the Dukes would fall out of their frames.

He knew, if he was honest with himself, that when Ilina took him round the house, he had been overwhelmed by the treasures it contained.

The pictures for instance comprised a much bigger and more impressive collection than he had expected.

The china, brought mostly from France by one Duke, was in itself so notable that he knew it would be hard to rival it anywhere in the world.

The snuffboxes encrusted with jewels, which had been bought or presented to the first Duke, besides over one hundred clocks that he apparently had had a special partiality for, were fantastic.

There was inlaid furniture with cabinets, chairs and tables of almost every period and one room furnished at the time of King Charles II was a poem of love knots and gold angels holding up crowns, while above them the ceiling depicted Aphrodite surrounded by cupids carrying garlands of roses.

'No one will ever see these things again as long as I am alive,' the Duke told himself.

He decided that he would make sure that his orders were not interfered with and, once the house was boarded up, no one would ever be permitted to enter it again.

Because he thought that he would take a last look at its treasures before he turned the house into a tomb, he rose from the chair and walked slowly from the study into the library with its shelves loaded with numerous books, which stretched from floor to ceiling.

There was a balcony that was reached by a small carved brass staircase and Ilina had told him that the books on the balcony were all concerned with the Bury family.

The Duke looked up at them and wondered if as a last gesture he should have them taken out into the garden to be burned.

A bonfire, he thought, would be very symbolic of his feelings and unless, which he doubted, every book was duplicated in some other library then even the records of the Burys would perish and soon be forgotten.

Then he told himself that first it would take a long time to remove them all and carry them out and there was no one else in the house capable of doing it except himself and Singh.

Secondly the bonfire would be really rather pointless without a crowd to watch the books going up in flames.

He felt, as he had felt for years, that he wanted literally to fight somebody over the way he had been treated by the Duke.

But the only person whom he could shock and horrify by his behaviour was Ilina, who was hardly in sporting terms up to his weight.

Quite suddenly it seemed to the Duke that he was not as elated as he expected to be at the fruition of his plans that he had waited so long for.

"I have won! I have won!" he called out aloud.

But the huge library seemed unimpressed and he walked out of the room and along to the Picture Gallery.

He had been to a Reception at Buckingham Palace before leaving England and he had thought that the pictures there, which had been collected by King George IV, were very fine.

Yet there was no doubt that the pictures in The Abbey equalled or even excelled them.

It was his mother who had taught him to understand art in all its forms and especially to appreciate fine paintings.

His father had sent him to Rome in his holidays from Eton and to Florence when he was at Oxford University.

When he looked at the collection of paintings that had been accumulated by the Burys over the generations, he knew that any Museum or Gallery would be proud to receive even one of them.

Far away at the back of his mind his conscience asked him if he was justified in denying to the world something that could never really belong to one individual but rather to every man and woman who appreciated beauty.

Then he told himself harshly that he would not be tempted to forgo his revenge and, leaving the Picture Gallery he walked into the Armoury.

This, he felt, was far more to his liking.

Here were weapons that had been used in battle including duelling pistols that various Burys had avenged an insult with and guns of every sort that they had pursued game with in England and in other parts of the world.

'It might have been more effective if I could have challenged the late Duke to a duel,' he mused. 'That is how feuds are settled in Italy and when the offender is dead then undoubtedly right triumphs.'

But Ilina had told him that her father had been a helpless cripple before he died and the Duke supposed that the man he should have fought would have been David his son.

But David had died fighting for his country, as scores of Burys had done over the centuries, which was the reason why he was here.

'I expect he was as detestable as his father,' he thought defiantly and strode on.

When it grew near to dinnertime, he wondered if Ilina would plead with him once again to save the house and the estate.

This would be his opportunity to explain to her exactly why he was so determined to have his revenge and the reasons why it was entirely and absolutely justified.

As Singh was helping him change for dinner, he was unusually silent because he was thinking over how he would present his case to her.

He would make her realise that the shocking way that his mother and father had been treated could be avenged, if not in blood, then only by the annihilation of The Abbey.

When he went downstairs to find that there was nobody in the study, he began to wonder what Ilina was feeling and if he had upset her so much that she would refuse to dine with him.

"Dinner ready, Master," Singh announced from the door.

"Where is Miss Ashley?" the Duke asked sharply. "Or rather Lady Ilina, which is her real name."

"Maid say Lady Sahib not come back," Singh replied.

"Not back?" the Duke asked. "Where has she gone?"

"Gone riding, Master."

It was what he might have expected, the Duke thought, that she would turn to her horse for comfort.

He had not been in Ilina's company without being aware of the almost human love that existed between her and Pegasus.

That she rode superbly went without saying, but there was also something else, which the Duke knew he had seen only in the East, where men could charm not only snakes but animals of every description because in some uncanny way of their own they communicated with them.

He was sure that this was what Ilina was able to do with Pegasus and he thought that she was undoubtedly relating to him with horror what he had said to her.

And strange though it might seem, he was almost compelled to believe that Pegasus would understand.

He ate dinner alone and found it annoying that he was not able to argue with Ilina as they had done last night while they duelled with each other in words.

He understood now that the expression he had not been able to identify in her gold-flecked eyes had been one of hatred and he found it distinctly unusual for a woman to hate him.

He had been so busy during the last few years that he had not had a great deal of time for women, but thinking back he knew that any whom he approached had fallen into his arms with an eagerness that was certainly flattering.

Even so his love affairs, if that was what they were, had never lasted very long for in fact he found that his work was far more interesting than any woman.

Although when he had the time they undoubtedly lit a fire within him, he thought cynically that it soon burnt itself out and work was a far more enduring excitement.

When dinner was over, fortunately Mrs. Bird did not realise that he had hardly noticed what he ate and had little appreciation of the culinary skill expended on it, the Duke walked back to the study.

He had hoped that Ilina might be waiting for him, but instead he found himself appreciating the vases of flowers and the fact, which was also her doing, that so many treasures had been accumulated in one place.

There were not only portraits of the Dukes on the walls, but an arrangement of miniatures also of the Bury family, some of them very valuable, hung on either side of the fireplace.

Several pink *Sèvres* vases on the mantelpiece were exquisite specimens that were irreplaceable.

The gold inkpot on the desk had been fashioned by a great craftsman in the reign of Charles II and the clock on the mantelpiece whose hands were set with jewels had come from France and had once stood in the Palace of Versailles.

So many lovely treasures that would never again see the light of day.

Because he wanted to shout the words aloud and make Ilina face the reality of them, it was annoying that he had no one to talk to except himself.

He threw himself almost petulantly down in one of the large leather-covered armchairs and stared with hostile eyes at the second Duke in his elaborate frame.

"You are a hero!" he jeered at him aloud. "But no Bury will ever forget me!"

He wanted to say it to the Burys who were alive rather than to those who were dead, so for a moment he played with the idea of giving a party at The Abbey before he closed it.

He would assemble all the Burys here and having told them what he thought of them, he would enjoy their abuse or their tears, when they realised what he intended to do.

Then he remembered that if he was to find the Burys he would need Ilina's help.

"Damn the girl!" he said aloud. "Why did she have to disappear just when I need her?"

It was dark by now and he knew that she must have returned and gone to her own rooms to avoid meeting him.

He thought of sending Singh or the housemaid, if she was about, to tell her that he wanted to speak to her.

Then he decided that, if she refused to come as she was very likely to do, it might make him look foolish.

Instead he could only sit alone, feeling that three of the Dukes who had preceded him were staring at him balefully and with the same dislike that he felt for them.

Because he was so lost in his thoughts, it was after midnight when, feeling a little stiff and slightly cold, he rose and, blowing out the candles, walked slowly through the hall and up the stairs to his bedroom.

The house was very quiet and he had told Singh not to wait up for him knowing that the man had been working all day to help the Birds.

"Is there no one to help you, Singh?" he had asked when he went up to change out of his riding clothes and found him brushing the floor.

"Nobody, Master," Singh replied. "Housemaid too old, others busy."

He had assisted the Duke to change, saying as he did so,

"Very fine house, Master! Very big like house of Viceroy, but needs plenty servants, many, many servants."

"I agree with you, Singh."

"Servants open rooms for big parties," Singh said with relish.

The Duke was about to say that it was something that would never happen when he thought that Singh might relay the information to the old couple downstairs and it would upset them.

The food was excellently cooked and he had no wish to have Mrs. Bird crying hysterically and ruining her dishes, while old Bird would be asking him where they could go if they were turned out of the house.

'They are not my problem,' the Duke said to himself, 'and I will not be side-tracked into worrying over people who anyway are too old to be working.'

He thought, however, with a twist of his lips that Ilina would doubtless demand that he should provide them with pensions and he supposed the same would apply also to Jacobs, the gardener and God knows how many others besides.

'The sooner I am away from this damned nightmare the better,' he thought and was aware because he was scowling that Singh, who knew his every mood, was looking at him apprehensively.

He felt now that the grandeur of his bedroom was somehow annoying and he undressed quickly and, blowing out the candles, settled himself to sleep.

Then, just as if he was being haunted by the other Dukes, who had slept before him in the great four-poster bed, he found himself arguing with them and defending his actions against their accusations.

'Nothing you can say will persuade me that it is not time the whole myth of the Burys' infallibility came to an end!' he told them.

It was then that they seemed to put forward what he had to admit were intelligent arguments that he could find no answers to.

As he tossed from side to side and lay unable to sleep, he decided that their faces were haunting him and he got out of bed.

He pulled back the curtains and found that the moonlight was flooding over the Park and the lake making the whole place seem enchanted and the Duke knew that until now he had not realised how lovely it was.

Because he felt that this was something else that he would never be able to forget he decided that he would go outside and ride.

Only by taking some sort of exercise could he free himself from the voices of his ancestors and the fear that if he was not careful he would be fighting a losing battle.

It took him only a few minutes to dress and then he walked down the stairs and let himself out through the front door.

*

There was no need for the candles, which had guttered out in the sconces, since the moonlight came through the high glass windows with the Bury Coat of Arms emblazoned on them in stained glass and cast weird patterns on the floor.

It also illuminated the tattered flags that the Burys had won in battle and which hung on either side of the huge marble fireplace.

The Duke closed the front floor behind him and walked slowly across the front of the house until he reached the stone arch that led into the stables.

The moonlight made everything as bright as if the sun was shining and he could not help appreciating the architecture of the stable buildings.

These had been erected at the same time as the first Duke had enlarged The Abbey and added the Palladian columns, the steps and the two wings that made it so impressive.

The moonlight also shone into the stables and he had no need for any other light to see the stalls where there were only two horses, Pegasus and Rufus.

Pegasus was first and he glanced into his stall to see that the horse was lying down.

But to his surprise Pegasus put back his ears and lifted his top lip almost as if he was snarling.

Then he realised that beyond Pegasus, lying on a mound of hay at the far end of the stall, was Ilina.

She was asleep and her horse was guarding her.

She looked very lovely, very young and very vulnerable.

The Duke could see the tearstains on her cheeks and one hand was flung out palm upwards towards Pegasus almost as if she was asking for the horse's protection.

The Duke stood looking at her for a long time thinking that, because she had disputed and fought with him, she had seemed in his mind to be as doughty and aggressive as an Amazon.

Yet now she appeared little more than a child with her fair hair curling round her forehead, her eyelashes wet and even in her sleep, which he felt was one of exhaustion, he saw that her lips trembled.

Then, as if he was determined to do what he intended to do, he went into the next stall.

He led Rufus out as quietly as possible and picking up the saddle from where it was hanging, took him outside to saddle him in the stable yard.

As he rode away, he had the feeling that he was escaping from something that was encroaching on him.

The Duke rode for a long way, following first the safe path through the Park and then galloping Rufus over the flat land until the horse was sweating and he felt as if some of the cobwebs had been swept away from his mind.

Only when he realised that he was quite a long way from home did he turn Rufus round and he told himself that the sooner he settled everything to his satisfaction and left England the better.

'If I stay here, I shall become sentimental and doubtless involved in a way that I have no wish to be,' he said to himself.

He had come back to England with a firm intention in his mind and nobody, certainly not a Bury in the shape of Ilina, was going to alter it.

"England is not for me!" he said aloud.

Rufus twitched his ears at the sound of his voice, but otherwise the Duke thought that it was a challenge that made no impact.

The moonlight made The Abbey, when he saw it in the distance, look like a Fairy Palace, magical and magnificent, and he found himself wondering what his standard would look like if it was flying from the roof.

He remembered his father telling him the reigning Duke's standard always flew there when he was in residence.

"Ridiculous frippery!" he exclaimed and rode on.

He restrained Rufus from going too quickly now that he knew that his stable was in sight and he would soon be back in it again.

There was no hurry the Duke reflected and there was no need to wake Ilina and have to make some explanation as to why he was out riding in the middle of the night.

Also he did not wish to ask her why she was sleeping in her horse's stall.

He knew that the answer was that there was no one else to whom she could turn to for comfort and no one else to whom she could cry, because the house she loved and which apparently meant so much to her was to become a ruined monument to the last Duke.

'I shall never marry,' the Duke told himself, 'in case I have a son, who might wish to inherit all this rubbish!'

Even as he said the words he saw the Van Dycks, the miniatures, the snuffboxes, the pink *Sèvres* and the books. Thousands and thousands of books and he knew that many of them contained eulogies of heroic Burys.

"They are dead," the Duke cried out. "There is nothing they can do except stay in their graves while I go on living and that will be the end! There will be no seventh Duke of Tetbury and as the years pass the Burys that are left will forget The Abbey and the estate that has become a wasteland for birds and vermin."

He drew nearer to the house and now he found himself hoping that Ilina had awakened and gone to bed.

He had no wish to see her now and no wish to talk to her and, if she cried, he told himself, it would merely irritate him as he disliked scenes of any sort.

Then, as he was riding alongside the lake, he saw her come walking through the gateway from the stables.

As she was a long distance away, he had the feeling that she was looking at the moonlight on the house, as he was able to do, and thinking how beautiful it was.

Then she stood very still and he wondered what she was thinking until unexpectedly she ran to the front of the steps that led up to the front door.

Then she stopped again and he saw that she was looking to the left of them.

Almost as if his eyes followed hers, he too looked left and saw that she was staring at a light in the study window.

It was little more than a golden glow and yet it was there and he remembered distinctly that he had blown out the candles before he went to bed.

'I must be mistaken,' he thought.

Then he saw that a casement was open and there was something strange beneath it.

The study was not at ground level, but as was usual in a Palladian house, level with the top of the flight of steps that led up to the front door and there appeared to be a rope hanging from the window to the ground.

Even as he stared at it, the Duke saw Ilina run swiftly up the steps to the front door, open it and disappear inside.

~110~

It was then, for the first time since he had seen her, that he sensed danger and spurred Rufus into a gallop.

CHAPTER FIVE

Pegasus moved.

And Ilina woke and for a moment could not think where she was.

The horse nuzzled at her. She patted his nose and, sitting up on the straw, realised that she had cried until she was exhausted.

Now she smoothed back her hair from her forehead and pulled some pieces of straw from it.

She felt calmer but at the same time had a sense of despair, which she knew would increase every moment until the terrible deed that the Duke contemplated was completed.

As the horror of it swept over her, she asked aloud,

"How – could he? How could he do – anything so – wicked?"

Then she realised that it was no good going back over it all again and the best thing she could do would be to go to bed and hope that in the morning by a miracle he might have changed his mind.

There was, however, not even a glimmer of hope in her heart because she had known since she first saw him that he had a vital determination and a sense of purpose in which he differed from most people she had met.

She was certain that, if he was determined to destroy everything that belonged to the Burys, then he would do it.

Even to think of it now she was awake, made her feel her own helplessness, that she was beating her head against a rock and the only thing that would be hurt would be herself.

"How do I make him see, Pegasus?" she asked, "that his desire for revenge is utterly unimportant in comparison with the achievements, the happiness and the inspiration that the family has given people – in the past?"

Then, as Pegasus could not answer her, she rose to her feet knowing that she could go on talking all night and it would get her nowhere.

She patted the horse, laid her cheek for a moment against his neck and then walked from the stall closing the door behind her.

As she came out into the stable yard in the moonlight, the glory of it seemed such a contrast to her own feelings of darkness and despair that she thought for a moment that it must be an omen sent by God to tell her that after all there was hope.

But, although instinctively her spirits rose for a moment, her brain told her that she had to face the truth however unpalatable it might be.

Slowly she walked across the cobbles of the yard through the stone arch and when in front of her she saw the Park, the lake and then the house, it made a picture that she knew however long she lived she would never forget.

It was so mystical and so ethereal that she thought that in all the years that she had lived at The Abbey, she had never seen it so beautiful.

Then she had eyes only for the house, thinking that on the Duke's orders the windows would soon be covered with boards, the great front door barred and it would be, as he had said, nothing but a tomb.

The treasures inside would rot and decay.

And probably by the time he died and someone could do anything about it, it would be too late.

Yet at the moment it was so lovely that it was part of her dreams and she walked very slowly towards the steps thinking that, if she never woke up, this was how she would like to die.

As her eyes moved along the house, she saw that there was a light in the study window and thought that the Duke must still be there where she had left him.

Was it possible that he was sitting there thinking that he had made a wrong decision or was he making plans for the workmen to come in and carry out his revenge?

She had never thought that anything like this might happen. Yet she had sometimes imagined that the Duke might never return to England.

When he did, she saw that he was obviously hard-up and there would be nothing he could do to save The Abbey unless he consented to her suggestion, which might be illegal, but was not unreasonable.

That he should seek such a savage revenge for the way that his father had been treated seemed so unbelievable that even now after she had heard him say it, and cried as if her heart would break, she still wanted to believe that she had been mistaken.

Even if he had no money he could do something for the estate, sell the timber for one thing.

Also once it was known that he was back and prepared to take his place as Head of the Family, perhaps some of the relatives would help.

At least they might restore the Dower House or some of the cottages.

As she thought of it, she gave a little cry.

'Was it possible? Could the Duke be meaning to leave England and return to the East without providing for the pensioners?'

She remembered that Mr. Wicker and his partners had been paying them until he returned and that meant another debt, which somehow would have to be met.

'If he will not sell the pictures,' Ilina reasoned, 'there will be no money to keep the old people from dying of starvation.'

There were also the Birds and Jacobs and Williams to be considered and she thought frantically that the fifty pounds that Mr. Wicker had put on one side for her would not keep them all for more than two or three months.

After that there was nothing but the workhouse, which she had always known decent people shrank from in horror and would rather die than be sent there.

'They *will* die!'' she said aloud.

She looked again at the lit window of the study as if she could send the words like a plea for help to the Duke.

She had reached the bottom of the steps and suddenly, as she looked at the open casement she saw something hanging from it to the ground.

It was a drop of about twelve feet and she saw trailing down the wall and onto the ground was a thick rope.

For a second the full significance of it did not strike her.

Then with a cry of horror she ran up the steps, opened the front door, and hurried across the hall.

Only, as she reached the study door, did she pause for a moment and think that what she was expecting was absurd.

There was no sound coming from inside the room and she was sure when she opened the door that she would find the Duke sitting either at the desk or in an armchair.

'1 cannot see him again,' she thought. 'Not tonight at any rate.'

Then, as she started to turn away, she heard a man's voice speaking and, because she had to know what was happening and who was with the Duke, she turned the handle.

The door opened and she gave an audible gasp.

Inside the room there were two men. They were dark-skinned and at one quick glance she realised that they were not English but had come from the East.

One man was at that moment lifting a miniature down from where they hung on the side of the fireplace and putting it into a sack with the others he had already removed.

The other man was standing at the desk with the gold inkpot in his hands and he stared at her in an ominous manner.

"What do you think you are doing?" she asked furiously. "How dare you come here and steal what does not belong to you?"

The man at the desk put down the inkpot and walked towards her.

"Are you Ilina Bury?"

He had a decidedly singsong voice and mispronounced her name, but at the same time was intelligible.

"I am Lady Ilina Bury," Ilina replied, "and you will put back those miniatures on the wall and leave the house immediately or I will call the servants and have you – taken before – the Magistrates."

As she spoke, with a sudden tremor of fear she knew that, if she called out or screamed, no one would hear her.

The servants slept too far from the study to hear anything that happened and, even as she confronted the two men, she was aware of how helpless she was.

"You the person we look for," the man said.

"Why? Why should you be looking for me?" Ilina enquired.

His lips twisted in his dark face she thought unpleasantly before he replied,

"You give us Nizam's jewels. That's what we want."

For a moment Ilina was too astonished even to feel afraid.

"The Nizam's jewels?" she repeated. "I don't know how you have heard about them, but they do not exist."

"That not true."

The man came nearer to her.

Now, as she thought that he might be going to lay hands on her, she turned, thinking that she must run away and escape.

But it was too late.

He put out his hand and caught hold of her wrist.

"Give us jewels. If not, you hurt."

Ilina gave a cry and twisted her wrist, but his fingers were like steel and the other man put down his sack and came to her side.

She saw that he was holding a sharp pointed knife in his hand.

"I promise you I am – telling the – truth," Ilina stammered insistently. "The Nizam's jewels that were – brought to this house many, many – years ago were – hidden and have – never been found."

"I make her tell."

As he spoke, the other man lifted his knife towards her face.

She shrank away with a scream and at that moment through the half-opened door came the Duke.

"What the devil is going on?" he asked furiously.

Without wasting time he brought his riding crop, which he held in his left hand, down with a slashing blow on the arm of the man with the knife.

He dropped it with a yell and the Duke punched him full in the face and felled him.

The other man moved quickly.

He released Ilina's wrist, put his arm round her neck and, holding her tightly against his chest, dragged her backwards.

Then he fumbled in the pocket of his coat and, as the Duke, having settled the man with the knife, turned towards him, he brought out a pistol.

"I kill you," he said and levelled the pistol at the Duke.

Ilina, with a compulsive movement of her right arm, managed to knock his hand upwards.

She did not think, she only acted instinctively.

As the man who held her pulled the trigger, there was a violent explosion and the bullet went wide, hitting the portrait of the second Duke that stood over the writing desk.

The Duke rushed forward as the man struck at Ilina with the pistol.

As she fell, her head caught the ornamented edge of the desk, a scream was stifled in her throat and she knew nothing more.

*

The Duke, having knocked the man with the pistol unconscious, tied him up with the cords he took from the sides of the curtains.

He then turned his attention to the first man. He was moaning and blood was coming from his mouth.

The Duke tied his hands behind his back before he picked Ilina up gently from the floor.

He was holding her in his arms when Singh appeared in the doorway.

"I hear shot, Master?"

"You did," the Duke replied. "These thieves were disturbed by her Ladyship and they fired at me."

Singh regarded the two Indian men on the floor, smiled and remarked,

"Master done well. They go prison."

"Tomorrow will be soon enough. Get more rope, Singh. There is some hanging from the window. Make certain they cannot escape. Then lock them in."

"I do that."

The Duke did not wait to see his orders carried out, but took Ilina out of the room across the hall and up the staircase.

She was very light and her face, when he looked down at her, was so pale that he wondered how badly hurt she was.

He knew that she slept in the West wing and he was relieved when he reached to find that there was a light burning in the passage and another inside a room where the door was open.

He walked into the schoolroom and guessed that an open door on one side of it would lead to a bedroom.

He was not mistaken and when he put Ilina down very gently on the bed, he fetched a candle from the sitting room so that he could examine what damage had been done to her.

Her eyes were closed, her face was ashen and he thought that there were still stains of tear-marks on her cheeks.

But there was also a flaming red patch on her forehead where the Indian had hit her with the pistol.

When he moved her head gently to one side, he found that there was blood on his fingers and on her hair at the back.

He was wondering what he should do when Singh came into the schoolroom.

"Can I help, Master?"

"Yes, Singh," the Duke replied. "Fetch either Mrs. Bird or that old housemaid to put her Ladyship to bed. Then have a look at this wound on her head. I am sure you are as good as doctor as anyone we can get hold of at this time of night."

"Leave to me, Master," Singh bowed.

The Duke looked down at the blood that was now staining the pillow behind Ilina's head.

As he had thought when he saw her in the stables, she looked very young, frail and vulnerable.

He wondered what would have happened to her if he had not seen her going into the house when he was returning from his ride.

Only Ilina, he thought, would have tackled the burglars alone without first fetching help.

He knew that was because she was defending the treasures that meant so much to her, treasures that he had told her he intended to destroy.

There was a strange look in the Duke's eyes as he sat waiting for Singh to return.

*

The following afternoon the Duke was in the study with Mr. Wicker.

There was no sign of the commotion of the night before. The miniatures had been put back in their place and the two thieves had been taken to the Police Station.

The Duke had discovered that the man who was ready to shoot him was a Parsee and a jeweller from Bombay and the other man a Muslim who lived in Hyderabad.

"I am afraid it is my fault that they came here in search of the Nizam's jewels," he said to Mr. Wicker.

"How can they have known about them, Your Grace?"

"When I received your letter informing me that my cousin was dead and I had inherited the title," the Duke answered, "I talked about it to my friends in Calcutta. I also told the story, because it seemed interesting, of the Nizam's jewels, which had never been found and which my father had told me successive generations of Burys had searched for unavailingly."

Mr. Wicker was listening intently but did not answer and the Duke continued,

"Everything in India is known and repeated. It was inevitable that the story of my inheritance and my predecessor's will should appear in the local newspapers."

"And those men decided to make the long journey to England to steal the jewels?" Mr. Wicker asked incredulously.

"The Nizam of Hyderabad has his own diamond mines," the Duke explained, "and is always spoken of as being one of the richest men in India if not in the world."

"If they had found the jewels, I suppose that their journey would have been worthwhile," Mr. Wicker remarked. "It would certainly be helpful in the present situation."

"If they are found, they belong to Lady Ilina," the Duke answered.

He had already explained to Mr. Wicker that he was aware of Ilina's true identity and the solicitor said,

"It would make me very happy, Your Grace, if the fifth Duke's legacy, which was made in what I may say was deplorably bad taste, could become a reality."

"How could he do such a thing?" the Duke asked.

"I am afraid, Your Grace, that we have to face the unpleasant fact that during the last years of his life the late Duke was not in his right mind. The way he treated his daughter was abominable. There is no other word for it."

The Duke did not speak and Mr. Wicker went on,

"When a girl of her age should have been going to balls and enjoying herself with young people, her life was nothing but a living Hell."

"There must have been relatives who could have helped her," the Duke said sharply.

"Her father would not have them inside The Abbey. He hated them all and Lady Ilina did her duty to him in a way that I can only describe as heroic."

"He certainly did not thank her for it."

"As I have said, Your Grace, the Duke was not in his right mind after his son was killed and he himself became crippled. But that does not excuse his behaviour and I can only beg Your Grace to help Lady Ilina, however difficult it may be for you to do so."

As he spoke, Mr. Wicker looked at the Duke's clothes as Ilina had done and thought that his hope that the new inheritor of the title might have been a rich man was as illusory as the Nizam's jewels.

As if he knew what his visitor was thinking, the Duke said,

"Perhaps Mr. Wicker, we should get down to business and you should tell me exactly what I owe your firm for managing the estate and for the pensions I understand you have paid pending my return."

Mr. Wicker took a deep breath and told him.

*

The Duke walked into the schoolroom to find Emily, the elderly maid, nodding in an armchair by the fireplace. She was looking tired and old.

She had been with Ilina all day, helped by Singh, who had carried everything upstairs that was required and had also bandaged the wound at the back of Ilina's head.

The old woman rose with difficulty to her feet as the Duke said,

"Go to bed, Emily. You have done splendidly. I am very grateful."

"Her Ladyship's still unconscious, Your Grace," Emily answered. "She's been a bit restless the last hour or so, turnin' from side to side."

"It often happens with concussion," the Duke replied. "As you know, the doctor said that there was nothing we could do but keep her quiet."

"I knows, Your Grace, but I ought really to stay with her Ladyship."

"I will do that," the Duke said. "You and Singh can look after her in the daytime and I will manage the nights."

He had said the same thing to the doctor, who had replied with a sigh of relief,

"If you can't manage, Your Grace, I don't know what I can do about it. I can't get a nurse for you. There's no one with any nursing experience here, except for a midwife or two. And they're not the sort of women that Lady Ilina should have about her. If we were in London it would be a different story."

"We will manage," the Duke said. "My man Singh is very skilled in treating wounds and has nursed me on several occasions when I have gone down with fevers, which I can assure you are not particularly pleasant in the East."

"So I have always heard," the doctor had said. "I'll come again tomorrow, Your Grace, and I promise you there's nothing we can do except hope that Lady Ilina will sleep it off."

He walked towards the door and, as the Duke accompanied him, he said,

"There has never been any young woman I have admired as much or who deserves more from the future."

The Duke did not speak and the doctor went on,

"Her patience and her devotion to her father are something I cannot even describe in words. All I can say is that if ever there was an angel on this earth, it's Ilina Bury."

"You knew her mother, I suppose?"

The doctor smiled.

"Another angel, Your Grace. One of the loveliest women I've even seen. There was no one who didn't adore her and her daughter has taken her place in the hearts of everyone who lives on the estate and in the villages round about."

If the Duke had not quite believed this, he had proof of it later that afternoon.

Singh told him that there were three children at the front door, asking for him. Surprised, he went to find out what they wanted and discovered that they were carrying huge bunches of flowers.

They explained to him that they had brought them from their mothers and grandmothers who lived in the village, but it was too far for them to come themselves.

However, signed on a piece of paper were the names of those who had sent the bouquets, three of them being only able to make a cross.

The Duke took the flowers and the oldest girl, who was aged about ten, said to him,

"Will you tell 'er Ladyship we wants 'er to get well quick and we all misses 'er?"

"I will tell her Ladyship," the Duke replied, "and I suggest that before you go home you see Mrs. Bird in the kitchen and ask if she has a piece of cake for you."

The smiles on their faces expressed their gratitude better than words.

Hurriedly they ran round the side of the house to the back door and the Duke was left with bunches of cottage flowers in his hands.

He gave them to Singh and told him to put them in Ilina's rooms.

Now as Emily shuffled towards the door, making an effort to curtsey as she reached it, he saw that there was one large bowl of spring flowers on the schoolroom table.

He looked at it, remembering what the children and Mr. Wicker had said.

Then almost automatically his eyes went to the picture over the mantelpiece.

There was no need for anyone to tell him who it was. There was a close resemblance to Ilina and also to the portrait of her mother in the drawing room.

The Duke looked at the smile on the young man's lips and the twinkle in his eye and, although he did not say the words aloud, he thought,

'He would have made a far better Duke than I am.'

He had brought up a newspaper with him, intending to read it in the sitting room.

The door into Ilina's bedroom was open so that he could hear her if she called out or became restless.

He decided first, before he settled himself for his vigil, to see how she looked.

He went into the bedroom.

The bed was that of a young girl with white muslin curtains falling from a corolla of small gilt angels.

The curtains over the windows, which were now faded, had, when they had first been hung, been bright with pink roses and bows of blue ribbon.

It was a very young room and the flowers in it seemed synonymous with its owner.

Ilina's nightgown, which fastened at the neck, had little frills of lace round the collar and on the sleeves. With her fair hair falling over her shoulders, she looked little more than a child.

Singh, with experienced skill had not covered the wound at the back of her head with a full bandage, thinking that if it encircled her forehead it would make her too hot.

Instead he had somehow managed to secure it at the back and told the Duke unless she was very restless, it would not fall off.

She looked as if she was asleep rather than unconscious and the Duke noticed that her long eyelashes were naturally dark against the whiteness of her skin.

Even so she did not look happy and he knew that he was responsible for the little drop of her lips and the faint line between her eyebrows.

He sat looking at her for quite some time and then, walking back into the schoolroom, he sat down in the same chair that Emily had found comfortable and picked up *The Morning Post*.

Jacobs had fetched it from the village, as the Duke had found that among all the other economies, Ilina had not been able to afford a newspaper.

He found himself uninterested in the English news.

After a moment he threw it down on the floor and sat back in the chair, his eyes going up to the picture above his head.

He wondered what David Bury, if he had survived and become the sixth Duke, would have done about the house and estate and the lack of money.

Would he, as Ilina had suggested, have sold the Van Dycks and the Holbein? But even the money from those pictures would not have lasted for ever.

Yet, if only one of the farms was put in order, it would mean some rent coming in every year and he supposed that the solution to every problem had to start somewhere.

At a sound from the bedroom the Duke hastily rose to his feet.

Ilina was, as Emily had said, restless. Now she turned her head first one way and then another and the Duke was worried that she would rub off her bandage.

Speaking for the first time since she had been injured in the study, she said in a frightened little voice,

"I must – go to – Pegasus. He is – starving – I know – he is hungry."

She tried to get out of bed, but the Duke put his hands on her shoulders and gently put her back against the pillow.

"He is – starving – I cannot – let him starve."

Then she gave a cry of horror and sat up again to say almost incoherently,

"Why – should we – starve? It's – easier to – die and be with – David. But Pegasus – how can I – kill you – when you are so beautiful?"

The Duke sat down on the bed beside her and put his arms round her.

"Go to sleep, Ilina," he suggested soothingly. "Pegasus is not going to starve and you must rest."

She made a little effort as if she would struggle against him and then suddenly she turned her head and laid it on his shoulder.

"Oh, David – David," she whispered, her voice almost inaudible, "I have – failed. He will not – listen, he is going to – destroy everything we – love. Everything – we have – left."

She gave a little sob and then in a voice that was somehow infinitely pathetic she said,

"Are you – angry with – me that I have – failed you and The – Abbey? Oh, David – I am so – ashamed that I have been so – stupid and ineffective."

Now she was crying.

The Duke could feel the tears shaking her whole body. She was still unconscious, but he knew that her skin was very hot because a fever was raging in her.

There was nothing he could do while she cried, but hold her close and hope that because she thought he was David it would somehow seem comforting.

Then she spoke again to wail brokenly,

"I have – failed – I have – failed."

He put her down very carefully against the pillows and squeezing out a flannel that was on the washstand in the corner of the room, he laid it against her forehead to cool it.

The mark where the Indian had struck her was burning, but, after several applications of the cold flannel, he thought that her temperature was not so high and she sank again into complete unconsciousness.

The Duke wiped her forehead with a towel and then pulled the sheet up to her chin.

Instead of returning to the schoolroom, he sat down by the bed on a small wooden chair watching her.

*

Ilina awoke, thought that she felt very strange and after a moment opened her eyes. She was in her room, but through the open door she could see that there was someone in the schoolroom.

It was morning, because the sunlight was coming through the uncurtained windows there, although in her own room the curtains were still pulled.

She wondered what had happened and why there was someone next door.

Then with a little cry of horror she remembered the man who had demanded the Nizam's jewels and the shot that had been aimed at the Duke.

At the sound she made, the person next door rose to his feet and she saw that it was Singh.

He came to the door of her room and asked,

"You awake, Lady Sahib? You understand what I say?"

"You are Singh," Ilina replied. "What has happened? Why are you here?"

Singh walked across the room and pulled back the curtains.

"You been ill, Lady Sahib. Have had concussion for four days."

"Four days!" Ilina exclaimed. "It cannot be – true."

"True," Singh affirmed. "Now Lady Sahib better."

He poured some liquid into a glass and brought it to the bed.

"Lady Sahib drink," he urged. "Nice barley water."

Ilina took the glass from his hand, feeling that it was an effort to do so and the glass was unexpectedly heavy.

After she had taken a few sips, she gave it back to him and lay against the pillows.

"Have you been nursing me?" she asked.

Singh nodded.

"Wound on head much better. Now fever gone Lady Sahib feel herself again."

"I hope so. Have you been sitting up with me all night?"

Singh shook his head.

"No. Master do that. He gone now take bath and sleep before he go riding."

Ilina gave a little exclamation.

"Pegasus! Is he – all right?"

"Master ride Pegasus every day. He very fine horse."

"Very – fine," Ilina agreed.

With a smile on her lips and her eyelids closing, she felt very tired, but somehow happy. The Duke was still here. He had not yet gone away.

Some hours later Emily came in with warm water for Ilina to wash and a fresh nightgown. It was one of her mother's and far more elaborate than her own.

Trimmed with lace it had narrow blue ribbons running through it, which ended in pretty little bows.

When Emily made the bed and brushed the front of Ilina's hair, Singh came back to dress the wound on her head and declare that it was very much better.

"Doctor say Lady Sahib very nearly well," he informed her. "Everyone very happy."

Emily had already told her that the vases of flowers, and by now there were over a dozen of them in the two rooms, had come from the village.

"Everyone very worried about you, my Lady," Emily said. "First the children came up with flowers and then Ben, the carrier brought three of the old ladies from the cottages to ask how your Ladyship was feelin'."

"How kind," Ilina said. "I hope someone was nice to them."

"His Grace saw them himself," Emily replied. "They all wanted to meet him. Your Ladyship can be sure they told everyone in the village what he's like."

Ilina gave a little laugh. She could quite imagine the chatter of tongues there would be!

Nothing had happened on the estate for years except the death of her father.

She knew that the story of the thieves climbing into The Abbey would be a wild excitement and that they had knocked her down would be something to talk about and exclaim over for years.

When Emily had finished and left her alone, she found herself thinking about the Duke and wondering if he had felt annoyed at having to sit up with her at night.

It seemed incredible that he should do so, but at the same time she realised that it would be impossible for Emily to look after her both day and night and Mrs. Bird was too old.

Gladys might be persuaded to help, but she could hardly work in the kitchen all day and then keep awake through the night.

That the Duke should have agreed to look after her was not only astounding but made her feel shy.

While she was thinking about him, it seemed almost as if her thoughts had conjured him up when she heard his footsteps first on the stairs and then in the schoolroom.

He walked to the door of her room and, as she looked at him, she stared wide-eyed for he looked very different.

So different that it took her a moment to realise that for the first time since she had known him he was dressed elegantly and smartly in well-cut clothes such as her brother might have worn.

"Good morning, Ilina," the Duke greeted her, coming towards the bed. "I have been told that you are awake, I began to think that you were the Sleeping Beauty and that cobwebs would accumulate around you for the next one hundred years."

Ilina laughed.

"I feel very – contrite," she said, "to have put – you to so much trouble."

"You have certainly been somewhat of a worry," he said in a dry voice and added, "does your head hurt you?"

"Not very much," Ilina answered. "Only the bruise on my forehead, which is very unbecoming, throbs a little."

The Duke sat down beside her bed and asked,

"How could you have done anything so rash as to tackle those thieves single-handed?"

Ilina blushed.

"I suppose it was very – silly of me. I did not stop to – think."

"It was most fortunate that I saw you going up the steps."

"So that is how you came at – exactly the – right moment," Ilina exclaimed and with a cry added,

"I remember now the man with a knife said that he was going to – cut off one of my fingers if I did not tell him – where the Nizam's jewels were – hidden."

"I heard the words 'Nizam's jewels' as I came down the passage," the Duke said, "and that was when I realised why they were there."

"If you – had not – come – "

"Forget it," he interrupted. "They come up to trial in a week or so and Wicker is sure that they will be sent on a convict ship to Australia or else be given a fifteen-year sentence."

"They – will not – be hanged?" Ilina asked, "Horrible though they were – I would not wish that to – happen to – anyone over me."

"As it happens they were intending to shoot me," the Duke answered. "If you had allowed them to do so, all your troubles might have been at an end."

Ilina found it hard to look at him.

She did not speak, but he saw the colour deepen in her cheeks and after a moment he said,

"That is not something we will talk about at the moment. Instead I will tell you that Pegasus is waiting impatiently for your return."

Ilina's eyes seemed to light up.

"He has been good with you?"

"He tolerates me, but he has made it quite clear that he prefers his owner."

Ilina smiled.

"I wish I could see him. I suppose he would find it difficult to get up the stairs!"

"I have a feeling it would be much more difficult to get him down!" the Duke answered. "It would be easier if you visited him as soon as you are well enough to do so."

"I feel so well. I am sure I can get up tomorrow."

"I am quite sure that Dr. Davison will not allow that," the Duke said, "but in case you are bored, he tells me that you are a good chess player and, as I rather fancy myself at the game, I am prepared to challenge you."

Ilina clasped her hands together.

"I would love that! Papa used to play with me – until he became too ill to do so. And David and I often played together when it was too wet to go riding."

"We will see how you feel tomorrow," the Duke promised.

There was a little silence and then Ilina said nervously,

"What have you been doing these – last four days?"

She felt that it was like waiting for a blow in case he declared that he had already started to board up the house.

Instead he rose to his feet, saying,

"I have had little time to do anything except worry over you, Ilina. And adjust myself to staying awake at night and sleeping in the daytime."

"It is very kind of you to – have done that and I am only – sorry I have been such an – encumbrance."

"There are better ways to express it and now I think you should rest. I will come to see you a little later before you are shut up for the night."

He walked towards the door and as he reached it, Ilina said,

"I am sure there will be no – need for – anyone to stay up with me tonight. If I do want – anything I shall be – able to get if for myself."

"Of course," the Duke replied. "Equally I am sure that when Dr. Davison arrives he will tell you that you must make haste slowly."

He stood waiting, as if he expected a reply and then she said,

"Thank you – again for being so – kind."

As she spoke her eyes met his. She felt that there was a strange expression in them that she did not understand.

Then, as he walked away looking extremely elegant in polished riding boots and breeches that could only have been cut by a Savile Row tailor, she found to her considerable surprise that she was no longer hating him.

CHAPTER SIX

"Checkmate!"

Ilina looked at the chessboard somewhat ruefully.

"You have won again," she exclaimed. "And I used to think that I was a good player."

The Duke smiled.

"I learnt many years ago with my father. Perhaps chess is a family pastime?"

"Why not?" Ilina asked. "As it may have been invented by the Chinese, it is always supposed to be a game for the intelligent."

"Is that what you think I am?" the Duke enquired.

Moving her chessmen back on the board, Ilina replied,

"I think you are very intelligent in – some ways and very – stupid in others."

She spoke without thinking and then, as if she felt that she had been rude, she looked at the Duke and apologised,

"I am – sorry. That was something I should – not have said."

"I like frankness," the Duke replied, "even if it is not very complimentary."

There was a little pause and then he asked,

"I suppose I need not ask the reasons why you think I am stupid, but I would still like to hear you say it."

"Do you mean – that?"

He nodded and she thought, sitting opposite him at the table in the schoolroom, it was difficult to imagine that any man could look so smart and at the same time so unlike what she imagined the gentlemen in London to be.

Despite the elegance of his new clothes, which she thought it would be too personal to comment on, there was something strong and vigorous about him.

His coat, like the one he had first appeared in, seemed of little consequence and it was almost as if everything he wore was just an adjunct to himself and subsidiary to his personality and character.

It was difficult to put into words, but he was so vital and so magnetic that she found it difficult to think of him as an ordinary man like her father or even David.

He might in fact have come from another planet.

And yet these last three days since she had ceased to be delirious and was agitating to leave her bedroom and go downstairs, he had been exceptionally kind.

Dr. Davison had been quite adamant that she was not to move too soon.

"Very little is known about head injuries," he said, "and the only thing I am certain of, having treated a large number of them from the hunting field, is that until the bruises have completely disappeared it is essential to keep as quiet as possible and let the body work its own magic to bring it back to normal."

"I don't – want to rest," Ilina said petulantly. "I want to go downstairs and – ride Pegasus."

"His Grace is doing that very competently for you," Dr. Davison replied, "and because I have no wish for you to turn suddenly into an idiot or a moron, I insist that you do not move from here until I allow you to do so."

Ilina gave a little chuckling laugh, which he thought was very attractive.

"I remember your saying almost those same words to me when I was about eight and had fallen off my pony. In fact, if remember rightly, you threatened either to tie me down to the bed or lock me in my bedroom!"

"You were lucky I did neither," Dr. Davison said. "As a little girl you were always hurting yourself in one way or another."

"I suppose I was adventurous," Ilina said softly, "something I have not had much chance to be since I grew up."

There was a shadow in her eyes as she thought of the long hours that she had spent at her father's bedside and the way that he had shouted at her and found fault with everything she did.

She often thought that the only thing that had saved her from going insane was Pegasus.

Because she was able to ride him early in the morning when her father was still asleep, or at any other time when his valet would sit with him, she could keep calm.

During those two years, which now seemed like centuries, she thought that without Pegasus and the love she had for him it would not have been her father who died but herself.

Now that the nightmare was over, only to be succeeded by another one, the problem that when the Duke closed The Abbey and she would have to decide what she would do and where she should go.

It was so much on her mind that she would go to sleep worrying about it and wake up in the morning asking herself the same questions for which there was no answer.

It would have been the same all through the day if the Duke had not come continually to see her and yesterday she had been well enough to move into the schoolroom.

He had brought up the old and rather battered leather chessboard that she had played on with her father and had challenged her to a game.

It had been an unexpected excitement, which had made her eyes sparkle and brought a flush of colour into her pale cheeks.

Because Dr. Davison had been adamant that she must not tire herself, she had worn a pretty dressing gown that had belonged to her mother.

It was blue satin a little deeper than her eyes and was trimmed with real lace, which the Duchess had taken from a ball gown she had worn when she was young. It made a wide frill round Ilina's neck and two rows of lace above her wrists.

It was too much effort to arrange her hair and she was actually afraid of getting tired so quickly that she would have to go back to bed. She therefore just tied it with a bow at her neck.

The sunshine streaming in through the windows encircled her head with a halo of gold. but she had no idea that she looked like a very young angel.

She felt a little embarrassed when she was waiting at the table with the chessboard in front of her for the Duke to come into the schoolroom.

She told herself that it was ridiculous to be shy when he had already seen her in bed night after night.

She was convinced that he was only waiting impatiently for her to get well so that he could close the house as he intended to do and go abroad.

They had played several games yesterday and now today, to her delight, he had come to the schoolroom after luncheon to play with her again.

She looked across the table at him and asked,

"Did you ride Pegasus – this morning?"

"Of course," the Duke replied. "I would not dare to face you if I had neglected your horse."

"Where did you go?" Ilina asked a little wistfully.

"A long way," the Duke replied surprisingly. "I found at the extreme North of the estate that there is a slate quarry."

"Yes, I know."

"I talked to some of the people in the village – "

"Little Fladbury?" Ilina interposed.

"Yes, Little Fladbury," the Duke agreed, "and they told me that there is still a great deal of slate in the seams. The quarry was closed down ten years ago because there were no orders for the slate."

Ilina was silent for a moment and then she said,

"I am afraid that was Papa's fault. He quarrelled with our Manager who I think was rather an incompetent man and after he had sacked him because we were hard-up, Papa did not replace him."

"So there was no one to find customers for your slate. That must, I suppose, also apply to the gravel pit."

Ilina smiled.

"So you found that too?"

"I consider it extraordinary," the Duke commented, "that anyone who was in need of money as badly as your father was, did not develop the natural sources of wealth that exist on his very large estate."

Ilina made a little helpless gesture with her hands.

"I am sure that you are right and I can only excuse Papa by saying that he was not a businessman or ever likely to be."

"Surely there was someone who could have advised him?"

"Perhaps Mr. Wicker and his partners might have done, but I am certain that he would not have listened to them. Mama loved him so much and wanted him to be happy, so she never argued or opposed him unless it was absolutely necessary."

"That is exactly how all women *should* behave to their husbands."

The Duke knew that he was being provocative and there was a mocking smile on his lips and a twinkle in his eyes that Ilina had begun to watch for.

"If a woman wishes to inspire her husband," she replied after a moment, "surely she should argue with him when she knows that he is – wrong or at least try to influence him in the right – direction."

Then, as if she felt guilty of criticising her mother, she added,

"I don't expect that Mama ever knew about the quarries. I knew only when I heard the servants talking."

"You did not think to mention it to your father?"

"Not until after Mama was dead and we were getting desperately short of money. Then I did suggest that perhaps the gravel pit might be put in working order."

As she spoke, Ilina remembered how her father had shouted at her to mind her own business and that when he wanted her advice he would ask for it.

He had added furiously that he was not going to sell anything that was his, as if he was nothing but a shopkeeper.

There was no need to express her memories in words, since watching her face the Duke was quite aware of what had happened.

"Of course," he remarked casually, "I am very out of touch with England and the way English gentlemen behave, but I cannot believe that all of them are so rich that if they had a goldmine in the garden they would ignore it."

As if what he had said took her mind away from the past Ilina laughed and replied,

"Not a goldmine, but I have heard that some lucky Noblemen own coal mines and that the Duke of Westminster receives an enormous income from the rents of the houses on his estate in London."

"Unfortunately I have not yet found coal or a built-up area on the estate," the Duke replied sardonically.

"I believe that my great-great-grandfather gambled away several streets and squares that belonged to the family," Ilina told him. "All that is left now are a few cottages that the tenants pay a shilling or two a week for and even forget to do that."

"And who collects those precious shillings?"

The way he spoke made Ilina look at him sharply before she responded,

"You know the answer to that. I am afraid that the cottages are in such a bad state and the people so hard-up I cannot – bear to take their money."

The Duke smiled.

"That is what I heard. If your father was a bad businessman, Ilina, you are certainly a very incompetent business woman!"

"I am aware of that. I suppose because I have always felt ashamed that we have done so little for our tenants, I thought that we really ought to pay them."

The Duke did not answer and after a moment she said in a very small voice,

"What will – happen to them when – you go away?"

As she spoke, she knew that part of her nightmare was the menace of the workhouse to those they employed.

There husbands and wives were separated from each other and most of the old people, when they were forced into the great gloomy building, were sure that they would never come out alive.

"That is something I have no intention of talking about now," the Duke said sharply and she thought he was afraid that she might argue and plead with him.

She was certain that he did not want to inform her again that his mind was made up and that he had no intention of changing his decision to go abroad and leave everything he had inherited to rot.

As if he was apprehensive that she might persist in saying what he did not want to hear, he rose from the table.

"You are not – leaving me?" Ilina asked quickly. "Please give me another game."

The Duke looked at the clock on the mantelpiece.

"I would like to," he answered, "but I have someone waiting to see me downstairs and I must ask you to excuse me."

"To see – you?"

It was a question but, although he must have been aware that Ilina was curious, he merely replied,

"I will come and say goodnight to you before dinner and to give you something pleasant to think about, Dr. Davison says that if you have a good night you may come down tomorrow for luncheon."

Ilina gave a little cry of delight.

"Did he say that – did he really – say it?"

"On one condition that you sleep well and you don't walk down the stairs or walk up them again."

Ilina looked at him questioningly and he said,

"That means, since Pegasus cannot oblige, I will carry you down and I have the feeling that you are even lighter now than when I carried you up here from the study."

He smiled before he added,

"That is really an order and you are to eat plenty for dinner tonight. I am going to tell Mrs. Bird that you are very hungry!"

"Oh – no! Please don't." Ilina exclaimed.

But already the Duke had left the schoolroom and she found herself talking to a closed door.

But she was thrilled at the news that, after being incarcerated for so long in two rooms, she could go downstairs.

Then, almost as if a shadow came over the sun, she found herself thinking that perhaps already the Duke had begun to board up some of the unwanted rooms in The Abbey preparatory to going abroad.

She knew instinctively that there was a kind of urgency about him these last few days that was different from the vibrations that had come from him before she was injured.

She was fully aware now that he had been both hostile and aggressive towards The Abbey and everything pertaining to it and at the same time completely indifferent.

He had seemed to her to be deliberately detaching himself from its treasures as if they did not concern him and he wished to have nothing to do with them.

'I don't think,' Ilina thought, 'I could bear to watch him destroying – for that is what he will be doing everything that I have loved and which, whether he likes it or not, is a part of us both and our blood.'

Then, as Emily came into the room to help her back to bed, she had to fight back the tears that came to her eyes and which she told herself angrily were a distinct weakness of hers.

*

When morning came she found to her surprise that, because she had been so tired when she went to bed, she had slept soundly and peacefully.

She had woken once in the night and prayed fervently that help would come from somewhere to save The Abbey and to make the Duke want to take his rightful place in England instead of going abroad.

'Please God – *please*,' she prayed, 'make him see that this is – something he – should do and stay where he is most – needed.'

She could not believe that any place in the world could need him more.

Yet she had to face the truth that it was not a very attractive proposition for a man who had no money and whose interests were all East of Suez.

'Yet because he is so clever, I feel that if he applied his mind to it he could make the estate pay and restore at least one of the farms,' Ilina argued with herself.

When she asked how she knew that he was so intelligent, she was sure that she could feel it from the waves that came from his personality, which at times she felt so strongly that they were almost overpowering.

Then she pulled herself up sharply.

What did she know? She was ignorant of men and certainly had met very few of them since she had grown up.

Besides if the Duke was really so clever, he would surely have made heaps of money abroad.

She remembered hearing of men who had acquired great fortunes in India, Singapore or Hong Kong.

'Why could he not have been – like them?' he asked, gazing up at the picture of her brother.

Then sensibly she told herself that it was no use crying for the moon. If there was no miracle to save The Abbey, then what she had to concern herself with was her own future.

"Help me, David – help me," she said aloud.

There was no reply and she thought that not only David but God had forsaken her and there was nothing she could do about it –

At the same time, because it was so exciting to go downstairs, she put on the prettiest gown she possessed and Emily helped her to arrange her hair in a chignon.

"Do you feel all right, my Lady?" Emily enquired anxiously when Ilina rose from the stool in front of the dressing table.

"My legs feel rather weak," she replied. "But it will be lovely to go downstairs and – "

She paused.

She had been about to say, 'to see what is happening', but she knew that it was the last thing she wanted to see at the moment and instead finished,

" – and see Pegasus."

"I thought you'd be thinkin' of your horse, my Lady," Emily said. "We're all real glad you're better and Mrs. Bird has cooked all your Ladyship's favourite dishes."

"I must try to get to the kitchen to thank her."

"If you do you'll have – " Emily began.

Then stopped, as if it would be a mistake to say what was trembling on her old lips.

Ilina looked at her in surprise, wondering what she would find in the kitchen.

But Emily had already turned away and was opening the door into the schoolroom. As she did so, the Duke must have come in from the passage for Ilina heard her say,

"Good morning, Your Grace. Her Ladyship's ready for you."

Ilina was about to walk into the schoolroom when he came into the bedroom.

Once again she found herself admiring his appearance and the smart cut of the frock coat he wore over a double-breasted waistcoat across which there was a gold watch chain.

Although she was ashamed of herself for thinking of it, she could not help wondering how much it had cost and where he had found the money.

Almost as if a little devil whispered in her ear, she wondered if he had already sold one of the pictures!

Then she told herself sharply that if he had, it was his business and it was not for her to interfere.

Nevertheless she could not help feeling a pain in her heart that accentuated whatever had seemed like a stone in her breast since the Duke's arrival.

It had grown heavier and heavier and at times she felt that it would finally stop her breathing from sheer fear and despair.

But, when the Duke smiled at her, the pain seemed to fade and she found herself smiling back.

"I am here to carry you out of your Ivory Tower. Are you prepared to face the world outside?"

"Yes – of – course."

"I would be very remiss, if I did not tell you that you look very lovely. Like spring itself."

Ilina stared at him in astonishment.

It was the first time he had paid her a compliment, but she told herself that he was merely teasing her and answered lightly,

"If you are feeling poetical – you have some – idea of how I am – feeling."

She turned towards him and he picked her up in his arms. As he did so, she felt a strange little quiver run through her, a sensation that she had never known before.

She then told herself it was because she was so excited at going downstairs. But, as the Duke carried her across the bedroom and through the schoolroom. she was very conscious of his closeness and the strength of his arms.

He walked along the corridor that connected the West wing with the centre block of the house.

Now Ilina was not thinking of herself, but was afraid of what she might see.

She felt that she must close her eyes just in case the boards were already up outside the windows and the hall was in darkness.

More probably, however, the Duke had started on the rooms that were not being used, like the Silver Salon and the Duchess's Drawing Room.

They reached the top of the stairs and, as he started to descend the carved and gilt staircase slowly and with care, Ilina realised that the sunshine was coming in through the long windows with their unstained glass and heraldic shields and illuminating the flags on each side of the big marble mantelpiece.

She looked lower and then thought that she must be imagining what she saw!

Because she was so astonished, she moved a little in the Duke's arms. He tightened them around her and, as he did so, she gave a gasp.

Standing on either side of the front door were four footmen wearing the liveried coats with shining crested silver buttons and striped waistcoats that she had not seen for many years.

She stared at them as if she was imagining their presence and then looked up at the Duke as if he would convince her that the scene was just a mirage.

There was a faint smile on his lips as his grey eyes met hers and she could only murmur in a voice that did not sound like her own,

"Why – are they – there?"

"They were what I expected to find when I arrived."

It was impossible for Ilina to say anything more.

He reached the last step of the staircase, moved onto the marble floor and carried her past the footmen towards the Silver Salon.

There was another footman, Ilina saw in astonishment, standing in front of the great double mahogany doors.

As they approached, he flung them open and the Duke carried her into the salon, which she had not seen without Holland covers over the furniture since her mother died.

Once again she was convinced that she must be dreaming.

The sunshine streaming through the windows as there were no shutters revealed the beautiful brocade and gilt furniture that had been designed by Robert Adam.

It also shone on the pictures, the china, and on the tables huge vases of flowers, which were very different from the little wild bunches that had been presented to her by the villagers, which had filled the schoolroom.

The Duke carried her to the hearthrug and set her down gently on soft cushions on the sofa.

When he had done so, he stood with his back to the fireplace, which was also filled with flowers and she could only stare at him in such surprise that her eyes seemed to fill her whole face.

"What – have you – done? Why is – it like this?" she asked in a whisper.

"You must tell me how it used to look," the Duke replied.

"It's lovely – lovelier than I remember. But I don't understand – "

He did not answer and instead went to a silver tray that stood on a table in the corner and filled a glass from a bottle of champagne that was resting in a crested ice cooler.

She sat looking at his back still feeling that she must be dreaming.

When she looked round the room again, she was sure that she must be asleep in the bed upstairs and that what she thought she was seeing was just an illusion.

The chandeliers, which had been grey with dust, were sparkling like diamonds.

Everything was so clean and polished so brightly that the colours that had been dim and dulled by neglect portrayed a freshness and a beauty that seemed to be part of the sun.

The Duke gave Ilina a glass of champagne and he had one in his other hand for himself.

"I think, Ilina," he said in a deep voice, "that this is where we drink to the future."

"The – future?"

It was a question and her voice trembled.

"The future," he repeated quietly. "May it bring you what you want."

Ilina looked up at him as if she was afraid that she was imagining what he had said.

Then, as if there were no words to reply with and she needed something to sustain her, she sipped a little of the champagne.

It was a luxury that she had not drunk since her mother had died and even before that only half a glass at Christmas and birthdays.

Now she thought that it was part of the sunshine and the glitter of the chandeliers.

When she at last found her voice, she asked,

"What is – happening? I just – don't – understand."

"We have a great deal to talk about, Ilina," the Duke said, "but for the moment I want you to enjoy yourself and to leave the explanations until later."

"How have you – done all – this and so – quickly?"

"I wanted to surprise you," he answered simply.

"You – have indeed. I was – afraid when I came – downstairs – "

"I know what you feared," he interrupted, "and now I am waiting for you to tell me all the things I don't know."

"What do you – want to – know," Ilina asked.

"For instance which of my ancestors brought the French pictures to the house, which one acquired the very fine snuffboxes in the cabinet over there and how which industrious Duchess was responsible for the exquisite *petit-point* on three of the chairs."

Ilina clasped her hands together

"Do you – really want to – hear about them?"

"I am waiting for you to instruct me."

Her eyes met his and somehow it was impossible to breathe.

Then the door opened and Bird announced,

"Luncheon is served, Your Grace."

He spoke in a stronger voice than Ilina had heard him use for many years and she thought, as he walked ahead of them down the corridor that led to the dining room, that he moved more quickly and with a new buoyancy.

Only when she reached the dining room on the Duke's arm did she understand.

Instead of just Singh to help him, there was a footman behind each of their chairs with two others in attendance by the side table.

It was all so bewildering that it became hard to think.

Ilina sat down at the table, which was decorated with flowers as her mother told her it had been in her grandfather's day. She was aware too that the finest silver ornaments were displayed.

'We are – using the Crown Derby – dinner service,' she noticed.

Then, as course succeeded course, she knew without being told that Mrs. Bird must have more help than Gladys in the kitchen.

The Duke was talking and she was listening to him wide-eyed.

"As soon as you are well enough," he said, "I want you to come to the stables."

"You know I want to do that."

"Not only to see Pegasus, Actually he is coming to the front door to tell you how much he has missed you before I take you upstairs again."

He saw by the expression in Ilina's eyes how much this pleased her and he went on,

"I thought and I am sure you will agree with me that Pegasus should have more friends to talk to than only Rufus. So the stalls are being filled one by one as the occupants arrive. And, of course, I shall require your approval of them."

Ilina drew in her breath and, because she found it impossible to speak, the Duke continued,

"I am unfortunately limited for space until the stables are fully repaired. Men have been working on them every day and I have offered them a bonus for speed. So I think you will be surprised at what has been achieved."

"I cannot – believe that – what you are telling me is true," Ilina said, when she could find her voice.

"I will prove it tomorrow," the Duke promised, "and after you have seen Pegasus there is just one more thing I wish to show you."

Ilina still felt sure that she must be living in an extravagant dream.

Only when luncheon was finished and the servants withdrew did she ask in a hesitating little voice, as if she was afraid to hear the answer,

"Tell me – why you are – doing this? How is it – possible?"

Sitting back in the high-backed chair with a brandy glass in his hand, the Duke looked at her with what she thought was a mocking smile as he said,

"What you are really asking, Ilina, is how I can afford it?"

"What – have you – sold?"

It was difficult to say the words because she was afraid of what she might hear.

"Actually nothing that belongs to The Abbey."

Then as she gave a little gasp, he asked,

"Why were you so certain I am a pauper?"

"I suppose," she answered truthfully, "it – was your clothes."

The Duke laughed, but now there was nothing cynical or bitter in the sound.

"Being a man I never thought that might be the explanation. I had been living in the North of Siam for nearly a year and was out of touch with what was happening in more civilised places."

"But I never thought of – that."

"Why should you?" he replied. "When I returned to Calcutta to find Wicker's letter informing of your father's death, I knew at once that I had to return to England immediately. I simply came on the next ship without waiting to smarten myself up."

Ilina gave a little sigh.

"It was – foolish of me to be so – influenced by appearances."

"But understandable and, of course, you had learnt what my feelings were about the title I have inherited and the Bury family as a whole."

There was a silence and Ilina looked at the silver ornaments on the table and the flowers as if she must reassure herself they were real before she asked in a whisper,

"Have – they changed – now?"

Again there seemed to be a long silence before the Duke responded,

"You saved my life, Ilina. I can hardly go on hating what matters so tremendously to you when I am exceedingly glad to be alive."

He put down his glass and then he said,

"Come, I have something to show you before we talk anymore and Pegasus, as you well know, dislikes being kept waiting."

Because she was so bemused by what he said and was also finding hope rising within her like a flame that leapt higher and higher, she tried to jump up from her chair.

She moved too quickly, forgetting how weak her legs were, and staggered.

Without saying anything the Duke picked her up in his arms as he had done before and, because out of sheer excitement the room seemed to be swinging round her, Ilina put her cheek against his shoulder and closed her eyes.

She felt his arms tighten as he carried her across the room.

The door had been left ajar and he moved it open with his foot and then proceeded down the corridor towards the hall.

Close against him Ilina felt that his heart was beating as strongly as hers was.

Yet she was desperately afraid that her imagination was running away with her and things could not be as wonderful as they seemed to be.

As they reached the front door, the Duke walked slowly down the long flight of grey steps to where Pegasus was waiting.

The old groom was holding him and, as the Duke put Ilina gently down on her feet, the stallion was nuzzling against her to express his delight that she was there.

She put her arms round him, saying in a voice that trembled,

"How are you – my darling? I have missed you – desperately."

He told her in his own way that he had missed her too and she saw that there were flowers on each side of his bridle and a garland of flowers around his neck.

As if he read her thoughts, Jacobs said,

"We had difficulty in gettin' him dressed up, my Lady, even though I thinks he knew he'd be seein' you."

"How are you, Jacobs?" Dina asked. "His Grace tells me that you have some newcomers in the stables."

"Ones you'll be proud to ride, my Lady, "Jacobs answered. "I now has four new grooms under me. I feels a new man."

At the proud and happy way he spoke Ilina suddenly felt that she wanted to cry from sheer happiness, but she was afraid that the Duke might see her tears and hid her face against Pegasus again.

As she did so, she felt the Duke pick her up in his arms again.

"Pegasus cannot have all your attention," he said. "There are other things to do and you will see him tomorrow."

There was a note in his voice that told her that he understood her feelings as he had never done before.

"Thank you – Jacobs," she managed to murmur.

As Jacobs led Pegasus back to the stables, the Duke carried her up the steps.

He took her along the passage that lead to the study and opened the door.

When they went into it, Ilina saw at once that there was a new carpet instead of the old threadbare one on the floor.

The furniture was shining as if a thousand hands had been polishing it for weeks and there were new satin cushions on the chairs and sofas, which, combined with the big vases of flowers that decorated every corner of the room, made the whole place seem somehow festive.

The Duke set her down on the sofa and, as she looked round, he said,

"I have ordered new curtains and I have brought you here to ask you which of the designs for the pelmets you prefer. I found when I looked at the sketches done for this room by Adam that he had made two alternative suggestions, neither of which, for some reason, was adopted."

Ilina took from him the sketches that he held out and he said very quietly as she did so,

"This room is more important to me than any other in the house for it is here, Ilina, you saved my life and here

I realised that I would not allow the thieves or anyone else to take from me what is mine."

Ilina drew in her breath and, as she looked up at him, he added,

"I also knew that it was impossible for me to leave you or lose you."

He spoke so quietly that for a moment she thought that she must have mistaken what he said and then he sat down on the sofa next to her and asked,

"You told me that you hated me, yet you saved me from being killed. I want to know what you feel about me now."

Ilina gave a little gasp and then, as she looked into his eyes, a strange sensation she had never known before seemed to start up in her breast.

It completely swept away the heavy stone of anxiety and fear and, rising into her throat, reached her lips.

She wanted to speak and yet it was impossible.

She could only feel the violent frantic beating of her heart and that the room was filled with a blinding light that came from the sky and yet was a part of the Duke and herself.

He drew a little closer to her, but did not touch her and after a moment he said,

"I suppose it was inevitable that I should fall in love with you and because I love you as I have never loved anyone in my life before, it is impossible for me to hate anyone. The past is all vanished and all I am concerned about now is the future, yours and mine, Ilina."

Then, very gently, as if he was afraid of frightening her, he put his arms around her and drew her closer to him.

He sensed that she was trembling, but not with fear and then, as she wanted to hide her face against his shoulder, he put his fingers under her chin and turned her face up to his.

"I love you," he breathed in a voice that was very deep and a little unsteady. "I have to know, my beautiful darling, what you feel about me."

She did not wait for a reply and his mouth came down on hers.

She knew that this was what she had wanted and, although she had not been aware of it, this was what she had been praying for.

At first his lips were very gentle and then, as if the softness of hers excited him, his kiss became more demanding and more possessive.

To Ilina it was as if he lifted her up into the sky and everything that had made her despondent and miserable and afraid had vanished.

She was no longer alone but part of him and the strength of his arms and the insistence of his lips gave her a security that she had thought would never be hers.

At the same time it was a rapture and an ecstasy that came from the Divine.

Only when she felt that she was disembodied and floating in space and there was music, the scent of flowers and the dazzling brilliance of the sun, did the Duke raise his head.

Then incoherently, as if the words burst from her lips, she said,

"I *love* – you! I know now – that I love you – but I did not realise it was love!"

"You love me," the Duke said a little hoarsely. "Oh, my precious, that is what I wanted to hear."

Now he was kissing her until it was impossible to breathe and, holding her so closely, that she felt she must have died and was in Heaven.

Then, when they both seemed to break under the strain of the wonder that was theirs, the Duke released her again and Ilina hid her face against his neck.

He could feel her breath coming in little gasps between her lips and her heart beating so violently that she was afraid it might fly out of her breast.

"I love you," the Duke exclaimed. "*God! How I love you!*"

He kissed her hair before he gave a little laugh and said,

"How could I imagine for a moment that I could really escape from what you believe is the call of our blood? But it is really all embodied in one small person, which is *you*."

"I love you!" Ilina exclaimed. "I did not know that a man could be so – wonderful – so exciting and yet at the same time want me."

"I will tell you how much I want you," the Duke said. "But first, my precious, we have to be married and as quickly as possible."

"M-married!"

"You may think I am too old for you, but because you have so much to teach me, and you have to inspire me to emulate the great deeds that the Burys have done down the centuries, the sooner we start the better."

There was no bitterness or resentment in his voice as there had been in the past.

Ilina gave a cry of sheer happiness and pressed herself a little closer to him before she said,

"You are not too old for me – but I am afraid that because I am so young and have done – nothing since I grew up except look after Papa and have seen – nothing of the world that you will – find me very – dull."

The Duke smiled.

Then, pulling her almost roughly closer still, he kissed her more passionately and more violently than he had done before, until he released her and said,

"Do you think that I want you to know anything except what I will teach you about love? And it will be one of the most exciting things I can think of to show you the world, which I will do, my adorable one, on our honeymoon."

She wanted to ask him a thousand questions, but he was kissing her again, kissing her until she knew that nothing she ever learnt, felt or saw could be as wonderful as what he was giving her now.

His love enveloped her and aroused a rapture that she did not know she was capable of feeling.

It was so perfect and so unbelievably wonderful that she could ask nothing more of the future than to be with him.

CHAPTER SEVEN

The Duke raised his head,

"I think, my darling," he said, "that you should go upstairs and lie down."

"I don't – want to leave – you," Ilina whispered.

Her whole body was throbbing with the ecstasy of his kisses and she was half-afraid that if she left him he would disappear in a puff of smoke and she would never see him again.

It was impossible to believe that what was happening was true and that, after all he had said and the misery she had passed through, he loved her.

She looked up at him and thought it impossible for any man to be so handsome and so mesmerisingly attractive.

"I love – you, I love – you!"

He held her close to him again and breathed,

"And I love you, my beautiful adorable one, but I want you to hurry up and get well so we can be married and be together for ever."

"That is – what I want – too."

He looked down at her and there was a tenderness in his eyes that she had never thought to see.

He then declared in his deep voice,

"You are so absurdly beautiful I want to stay here and kiss you and go on kissing you for the rest of the day."

Then he took his arms away from her and added,

"Instead I am going to think of you and I also have some rather important people waiting for me."

"Important?" Ilina queried.

"One of them has come to mend the picture of the second Duke that received the bullet that, but for you, would have killed me."

Ilina gave a cry of horror.

"Supposing that had – happened! Supposing I had not been – able to – save you!"

"But you did," the Duke smiled, "and I am having that bullet dipped in gold and I shall wear it on my watch chain for luck."

"It was very – very lucky for – me."

"And for me, my darling."

He kissed her forehead and then urged her,

"Come along, I am going to take you back to bed or Pegasus will wait for you in vain. And so shall I."

Ilina flashed him a smile before she answered,

"I will do as you say, because I know that you expect women to be obedient and subservient."

The Duke laughed.

"I very much doubt that is what you will be, but I love you just as you are."

He would have picked her up in his arms to carry her upstairs, but Ilina prevented him, saying,

"One moment – I just want to look at the picture. I am so very – very grateful that it was the Second Duke who was injured and not – you."

She moved round the desk as she spoke and the Duke said,

"Actually the bullet went into the corner of his frame. He himself was untouched, which you may say was the luck of the Burys."

"He was certainly lucky," Ilina said, "but I wish we knew where he had hidden the jewels."

She looked up at her great-great-grandfather as she spoke and saw for the first time that there was some resemblance in his features to those of the man she loved.

Then, because she could see that the Duke was waiting impatiently, she looked at the frame.

She saw that the bullet she had diverted had hit the corner of it.

It had dislodged a large piece of the gilding, which she saw lying by the blotter on the desk.

She looked at the frame and then gave a little exclamation,

"That is strange! Papa always said that most of the family portraits, especially those of the Dukes, were framed in wood carved from trees on the estate and then gilded."

"Is this one different?" the Duke asked.

"You can see that this is plaster," Ilina replied. "I wonder why we have never realised it before."

She looked at the white powdery mess left at the corner of the frame from which the gilt design had broken away.

There was a large lump in the middle of it and she licked her finger to rub it, thinking that there would be wood underneath the plaster that had been added later.

As she rubbed the white plaster, it crumbled away and then instead of the wood she had expected, there was something that sparkled in the sunshine.

She stared at it for several seconds and then gave a cry that seemed to echo round the walls of the study.

"What is it? What is the matter?" the Duke asked from behind her.

In a voice that trembled and seemed curiously unlike her own, she stammered,

"I think – but it seems incredible – I have found the Nizam's – jewels!"

*

The ship was moving on a smooth sea and it was very early with only the quiet rhythm of the engines to wake Ilina.

As she came back to consciousness, she realised that her head was on her husband's shoulder and that he was fast asleep.

The sunshine streaming through the curtains that covered the portholes was golden. She thought it symbolic of her happiness and the glory and wonder of her life ever since she had been married.

Every day, although she thought it impossible, she loved the Duke even more than she had already.

Every night he brought her a deeper realisation and understanding of love that made her realise that she still had so much to learn.

'How can he be so wonderful?' she asked herself now.

She knew that the ecstasy that they had found together was so spiritual and so Divine that he lifted her into a special Heaven where there was nothing but love.

'I am so lucky, so very, very lucky,' she thought.

Because of the intensity of her feelings she could not help turning her head to kiss the Duke's shoulder.

Without opening his eyes he moved his arm to hold her more closely to him and she kissed him again.

"I love – you," she whispered.

The Duke opened his eyes to look at her and in the dimness of the cabin she looked very lovely and very ethereal.

Her fair hair was falling over her shoulders, her blue eyes were gazing up to his and her lips were parted.

"How can you be more beautiful every time I see you?" he asked.

Ilina gave a little laugh.

"I have just asked myself how it is possible that I love you more every – morning than I did the – previous day."

"Is that true?"

"You know I would only tell you the truth."

He put out his other hand and touched the softness of her cheek and then ran his fingers along the line of her pointed chin.

As always when he touched her, it gave her a strange feeling like little shafts of sunlight running through her and she felt her heart begin to beat quickly and knew that his was doing the same.

"Today we reach Calcutta," he said, "and I must warn you, my darling, that, as you insist on my being so important, we shall be guests of the Viceroy and I only hope you will enjoy all the pomp and circumstance."

"I want you to be aware of your own importance," Ilina answered, "although at the same time I admit that I would rather be alone with you."

She thought as she spoke that nothing could have been more perfect than their honeymoon, which had been spent on the ship, where no one could disturb them unless they wished it.

The Duke had, as he had promised, taught her about love.

From the very moment he had kissed her, she had known that never again need she be afraid of the future and that the miseries of the past had disappeared like a mist vanishing before the sun.

Even the finding of the Nizam's jewels had not been as exciting as the Duke's kisses.

Yet it had been a thrilling moment when she realised that they were underneath the plaster that had been added to the original wood of the frame and then covered with gold leaf.

The Nizam's jewels had been indeed safe ever since the second Duke had hidden them there.

'How could he have thought of anything quite so ingenious?' Ilina asked.

They had peeled away the plaster that had been shaken by the bullet and found beneath it diamonds, emeralds and rubies that were so large that the Duke thought it would be difficult to put a value on them.

The beading round the frame, which was different from the frames of the other Dukes, concealed, of course, the Nizam's pearls.

The Duke and Ilina removed as many as they could until he said that it would be a great mistake to do it in a hurry and perhaps scratch the pearls and damage the other stones.

Nevertheless there was quite a large pile of jewels on the desk which, because they were all caked with plaster, the Duke had laid on one of his fine linen handkerchiefs.

Ilina's eyes were shining like the diamonds as she said to him,

"I cannot believe it! When I think how David and I searched attics, the cellars, the Chapel and every other place in the house only to be disappointed – "

She gave a laugh that was almost a sob as she added,

"Once we took most of the books out of the shelves in the library, thinking that the Duke might have hidden them there."

"It was certainly a very clever idea of his," the Duke agreed.

Then, as if she was overcome with the excitement of her discovery, Ilina threw herself against him to hide her face against his shoulder to murmur in a voice that broke,

"There are so – many things we can do now – for the people who have been – loyal to us all through the – bad days."

"I have already been thinking about that and I think you will find, my darling, that you can keep your jewels for yourself because I have quite a considerable fortune, which actually I have made by the sweat of my brow."

Ilina gave a little laugh and he continued,

"It's true. And I am still rather angry with you for being so sure that I was a pauper just because I was badly dressed."

"I am – sorry," she whispered, "and you do look so – very different now."

"Nevertheless," he said, "I am mortified to think that, while the Prince in the Fairytale recognised Cinderella in her rags and tatters, you took me just at my clothes' value."

She knew that he was teasing her because he did not want her to be emotionally upset by the jewels she had found, thinking that it might be too great a strain after her injury.

With a lilt in her voice she said,

"The last cloud has vanished over the horizon and now there is only – sunshine for us – both ahead."

"You can be quite certain of it," the Duke agreed, "but at the same time sunshine, jewels or anything else, I am going to carry you upstairs and you are to *rest*."

He accentuated the last word and, as Ilina made a little grimace with her small nose, he said,

"You want me to be authoritative and behave like a Duke, so I expect you to obey me."

She laughed.

He picked her up in his arms and looked down at her with such tenderness in his eyes that she felt her heart turn over in her breast before he said,

"I told you not to be too light in my arms. I also ordered you to eat much more than you are doing already and forget the days when you felt that you could not pay for it."

"It is difficult to – believe that they are – really over."

He turned her round so that she was looking at the picture of the second Duke.

"We should thank him," he sighed, "for having kept his treasure intact for so long. Now he knows that it will not be spent on gambling or riotous living."

He kissed her forehead and added,

"As your husband I shall make quite sure that it is not invested in dud companies or thrown away on wild schemes that always fail at the last moment."

Ilina could not help thinking that he was right and that, if her grandfather had found the jewels, he would undoubtedly have spent the proceeds on wine, women and horses and her father, after her mother died, would have done the same with anything that was left.

As it was, she could already think of a million things that required doing on the estate and which would mean new lives for those who relied on it for a living.

There would be plenty of work for young men and women who otherwise would drift into the industrial towns and of course, the house itself would become the focal point not only for this generation of Burys but for those to come.

As if the Duke, following the expression in her eyes, knew exactly what she was thinking, he remarked quietly,

"That is what I have begun to do, but, of course, my darling, I need your help and I cannot manage without it."

Because his need of her gave her such a warm feeling of happiness, she put her arm round his neck to draw his face down to hers.

"You are just preventing me from taking you upstairs," he said accusingly.

He kissed her lightly on the lips and then walked across the room.

As they proceeded down the passage into the hall, Ilina felt as if everything was shining with the light of happiness that seemed almost dazzling.

'How is it possible?' she wondered.

As if with the wave of a magic wand, the Duke had changed from the man she had hated and who had decided to make The Abbey a tomb for the treasures it contained to the man who seemed to vibrate with love with every word he spoke.

She put her head against his shoulder and thought that the miracle she had prayed for had happened and God had answered her prayers.

Perhaps David had known all along that things would come right.

When they reached the top of the staircase, the Duke turned her round so that once again she could see the hall bathed in sunshine and the footmen on duty in the front door.

Then, as she tried to find words to tell him how wonderful it all was, he moved along the corridor that led to the West wing.

As he walked slowly, carrying her as if she was infinitely precious, she asked,

"How did you manage to prevent anyone from telling me of the surprises you were planning for me?"

"It was not difficult," he replied. "Everybody in the house loves you and, when I told them what I was doing, they understood that I wanted to make you happy – "

"How many people have you given Mrs. Bird in the kitchen?"

"I have lost count," the Duke smiled. "When she realised that she could have as many as she wanted, every day she has demanded extra women in the kitchen, the scullery, the stillroom and the dairy."

Ilina laughed.

"You have to entertain lavishly to keep them all busy."

"That is what I intend we shall do when we come back from our honeymoon."

She looked at him enquiringly and he said,

"I think you have had enough excitement for today. You must leave me some more fireworks for tomorrow, otherwise you might be disappointed."

"How could I ever be – disappointed in – you?"

As if he could not help himself, the Duke stopped again and kissed her.

Then, as if he forced himself to walk on, he carried her into the schoolroom and set her on her feet in the bedroom.

She looked at him and, as she wanted to say once again how wonderful everything was, he pulled her almost roughly into his arms.

He kissed her until it was impossible to think, only to feel that the miracle she had prayed for was love and it was love that had changed everything and especially the Duke.

By the time the Duke had sent for Emily to help her into bed she was really very tired.

When Emily answered, she brought with her a very nice looking younger woman whom she introduced as 'Rose'.

"Now you know His Grace's secret, my Lady," she said, "I want you to meet Rose, who'll be takin' my place with four housemaids under her."

"You are going to retire, Emily?" Ilina asked.

"Just as soon as His Grace has a cottage ready for me," Emily replied. "And it's bein' done up regardless of expense."

The pride in the old woman's voice was very touching and Ilina said,

"Whatever it is like, Emily, you deserve it for being so wonderful in the bad times. Of course I want you to share in the good ones."

"And real good they'll be too, my Lady," Emily said, "just like when His Grace your grandfather were alive."

Ilina could not help thinking that it was her grandfather's extravagance that had left her father so impoverished.

But she told herself that the past was the past and not only was the Duke rich enough to restore The Abbey to what it had been but now she had the Nizam's jewels she herself was very wealthy.

It seemed incredible after they had hardly enough to eat and had to rely on the rabbits that Jacobs caught in his snare.

When Emily and Rose left her, she had lain back against the pillows saying a fervent prayer of thankfulness which was more a paean of praise for what had happened.

Yet she knew that more important than the Duke's fortune or the Nizam's jewels was that she had found love.

She tried to express her feelings to the Duke when he came to see her before dinner.

He was looking so magnificent in his evening clothes that for a moment she could only stare at him. Then, as he put out his hands towards her, she lifted her lips to his.

He sat down on the bed and kissed her until her eyes were shining, her cheeks were flushed and her breath was coming quickly between her lips.

"Are you not tired, my darling?"

"Only – excited."

"As I am."

"Do I really – excite – you?"

"I will answer that question when we are married," he replied. "Until we are, my precious love, don't tempt me because I am afraid of frightening you and making you hate me again."

"That will – never happen."

"You are sure?"

"Quite sure! I love you until you – fill the whole world – and nothing else is of any consequence."

"Not even the jewels," he teased, "that you can festoon yourself in like the Queen of Sheba?"

"It is very thrilling to have found them," Ilina answered him.

"I cannot think now why David and I did not think of such a clever hiding place. I long to be able to tell him – about it."

"I am sure he knows," the Duke commented quietly.

She looked at him in surprise, feeling that this was something that she would never have expected him to say.

As if he knew what she was thinking, he said,

"I have lived so long in the East that I believe in the *Wheel of Rebirth*, which is why we found each other again and that there is no such thing as death."

Ilina made a little murmur of happiness and, as she hid her face against him, he said,

"I have so much to teach you, my precious one, and we have so much to learn about each other that it will take a century to do so and the sooner we start, the better."

"I want it to start – now."

"Actually the real beginning will be the day after tomorrow," the Duke said, "when we are being married."

She looked at him in astonishment and he went on,

"I have already been to see the Vicar, who, as you know, is a very old man. He remembered your mother and spoke of her so warmly and with such affection that I know he will make our marriage a very real Ceremony to both of us."

Ilina put her arms around his neck.

"How could you be so marvellous? How did you know that is what I should want? And I am sure we are being married here in the Chapel."

"Of course," the Duke replied. "I have already put a dozen people to work on it and with masses of flowers it will be the perfect place where we will make our vows."

Because there were no words to express what she was feeling, Ilina kissed his cheek.

Instantly the Duke's arms tightened round her and there was a fire in his eyes and on his lips that had not been there before.

He kissed her until she was once again lifted into the sky and the world was left behind.

Then he put her back against the pillows and said in a voice that was unsteady,

"I told you not to tempt me. I want to stay here kissing you all night and making sure that you are mine, but I have a great deal to see to before the day after tomorrow."

He rose to his feet, but Ilina held on to his hand.

"Promise you will not vanish when you leave me and I shall not wake tomorrow morning to – find you have gone."

"I promise you I shall be here and loving you," he answered.

*

On the morning of the Wedding, Ilina found one of the things that had preoccupied the Duke's attention had been to provide her with a Wedding gown.

A number of other gowns had also been brought from London by train to the nearest Station and then carried in a brake drawn by four of his new horses to The Abbey.

With very small alterations, which were made by Rose and the new housemaids, they fitted her.

She could hardly believe when she put on her Wedding gown that she had a bustle as large as those she had seen illustrated in *The Ladies Journal* and never thought to own.

There was a veil that might have been made by fairy fingers and a wreath that was not of orange blossom, as she expected, but of diamonds.

It was only later she found that Singh, who knew exactly what the Duke wanted, had been sent to London to bring back a jeweller from Bond Street with a selection of tiaras from which the Duke could choose.

She was surprised at the speed he had got all that he wanted.

She was also astonished when she went downstairs on the day of her Wedding to see how much had been accomplished since he had begun to reorganise and redecorate The Abbey.

There were painters, carpenters and upholsterers in every room and the Chapel was, as the Duke promised, filled with so many flowers that it was impossible to see the ravages of time and that there were still many months of work to be done just in the Chapel.

As they knelt before the altar that had been consecrated when the Chapel was built over two centuries ago, Ilina felt that there were angels singing in the painted ceiling overhead.

Afterwards they had gone into the Silver Salon and, as the old Vicar toasted them in champagne, he said,

"I know that God will bless you both and it's a very happy day for us all. It's wonderful to know that Your Grace will make The Abbey as beautiful as it used to be and that our people can turn to you for help and guidance at all times."

Ilina drew in her breath and looked at the Duke, her eyes filled with love, and he replied quietly,

"My wife and I, when we return from our honeymoon, Vicar, have many plans to help the people who work for us."

"Is it really true, Your Grace," the Vicar asked, "that the school will be open again?"

"There will be schools in every village on the estate," the Duke answered. "And I have already written to the Bishop for suggestions of young Priests to fill the empty

Livings. I also think it is important that the orphanage should be modernised and enlarged."

Ilina clasped the Duke's arm and she knew that her hands told him better than words what she was feeling.

Only when the Vicar had left and the Duke had given orders that the villagers should be given beer and cider to drink their health, did she say,

"How could I ever imagine for a moment that you would not know how to – behave as a Duke!"

She was teasing and yet there was a hint of tears in her voice because she was so happy.

"I am sure that I will do a great many things that you will not hesitate to tell me are wrong!"

She laughed and put her cheek against his shoulder with a little tender gesture as she said,

"I have the feeling that I shall be telling you over and over again that you are perfect and in consequence you will become very conceited."

He laughed and kissed her and then astonished her by telling her his plans for their honeymoon.

Afterwards she felt that he conveyed her not by train and ship but by a magic carpet to Paris.

There he bought her so many exquisite gowns that she protested that the ship which was to carry them to India would sink from the weight of her luggage.

But when they boarded the P & O Liner at Marseilles, Ilina knew that every man on the ship looked at her and looked again in admiration and it gave her a confidence in herself that she had never had before.

What was so perfect was to be alone with the Duke and for him to make love to her until she was no longer the worried insignificant girl that she had been, but the radiant Goddess that he believed her to be.

"I have sought for you all my life," he sighed, "in pictures and sculpture, in music and on the snow-coated peaks of the Himalayas, but I was quite sure that you did not exist except in my imagination."

"Supposing I – disappoint – you?"

"You will never do so, my lovely one. Every time I look at you and every time I touch you I grow more and more in love. I know as surely as if the Gods themselves told us, we have belonged to each other since the very beginning of time."

"That is what I want to believe. You must teach me about what you call the *Wheel of Rebirth* so that never again will I be afraid or – want to die."

The Duke remembered what she had said when she was delirious and held her close against him as he said,

"How could you not have known that you belonged to me? And how could I imagine for one moment that I could escape my Karma, which is *you*?"

Then he kissed her and it was impossible to say anything more and the flames of love rose higher and higher until they touched the peaks of ecstasy.

Ilina knew that they were indeed one, now and for ever.

But what he had said to her was always in her mind and with her arms round him and her head on his shoulder, she enthused,

"I am very excited at the thought of being in India with you. How long will we be staying?"

It was a question that she had not asked before because she was half-afraid of the answer.

Although in a way she wanted her honeymoon to go on forever, her thoughts were always with The Abbey and the people who were waiting trustingly for their return.

As if he knew exactly what she was thinking, the Duke said,

"There are a great many parts of the world I want to show you. Not only India but Siam and Singapore."

He saw the question in Ilina's eyes and he went on,

"But because, my darling, you have made me very conscious of my consequence in England, I know that we cannot be away for too long."

Ilina gave a little sigh of relief and said,

"I want you to feel like that because sometimes when I am so happy – so ecstatically happy – I feel guilty that there are still people suffering on the estate through matters that are wrong and that only you can put right."

"I know what you are saying," the Duke agreed, "but I have left two very competent men in charge, who among other things will reopen the slate quarry and the gravel pit and thus employ a great number of young men who otherwise would leave for the towns."

Ilina did not interrupt, but he knew because she pressed herself a little closer against him that this was what she wanted to hear.

"At the same time," the Duke added, "I know, although you have not said so, that there are Hereditary Duties, both in the County and at Court that your father neglected and which I must undertake for the family's sake."

There was just a final touch of mockery in the way he spoke, but Ilina knew that he was not being bitter or cynical.

He was only laughing a little at himself and the idea of someone who had been ostracised by the Bury family now being instrumental in restoring their traditional high standing and influence.

"That is what I want you to do," Ilina said. "Oh, darling, nowhere could there be a more handsome or distinguished-looking Duke."

She paused before she asked,

"You will enjoy it?"

She was afraid for a moment that he would not answer and then the Duke said,

"Before you turned my world upside down, I was perfectly content to be a trader on a very large scale. That is how I made my fortune and I certainly enjoyed the years I spent in strange lands like India, Siam and Burma."

Ilina held her breath before he finished,

"But now I have every intention not only of enjoying my life as a Duke but of fighting for all the things you believe in, my beloved wife, and perhaps embellishing the family name as efficiently as all those ancestors you admire so fervently."

"I admire no one more than you," Ilina said quickly, "and because of what you said I not only love and adore you but admire and honour you."

She went on in a low voice,

"Only a very great man would have changed his mind as you have done in order to do what is – right and – noble because it is expected of – him."

She spoke intimately and with a little rapt note in her voice that the Duke did not miss.

Then, because she was so lovely and so utterly adorable as she looked up at him in the light that was growing in the cabin with the rising sun, he drew her closer still and his mouth sought hers.

As he kissed her, Ilina felt as if this had all happened before not in this life but in many others and their love was as old as time and as young as the future that drew them irresistibly to the heights within themselves.

This was their destiny and their Karma and she was sure because they were together and so happy that they would make the world a better place for others less fortunate.

"I love you," she murmured against the Duke's lips. "You are wonderful – perfect and you fill the world – and the sky. I know now you have taken me to Heaven – which is filled with love."

"Darling, that is what I want you to feel and because I love you, I will dedicate my whole life to your service and attempt to do everything you ask of me."

As he spoke, he raised himself to look down at her and then slowly, as if they had all Eternity in front of them, he sought her lips again.

She felt her heart beating against his and knew the fire that rose within them both was sanctified and came from a love that was so perfect it was part of God.

At the same time it was a love that created life.

As the Duke made her his, Ilina prayed that she might give him a son who would carry on the family and the glorious achievements that were part of their history as well as the country that they belonged to and loved.

OTHER BOOKS IN THIS SERIES

The Barbara Cartland Eternal Collection is the unique opportunity to collect all five hundred of the timeless beautiful romantic novels written by the world's most celebrated and enduring romantic author.

Named the Eternal Collection because Barbara's inspiring stories of pure love, just the same as love itself, the books will be published on the internet at the rate of four titles per month until all five hundred are available.

The Eternal Collection, classic pure romance available worldwide for all time.

Made in the USA
Middletown, DE
29 June 2021